J. T. EDSON'S
FLOATING OUTFIT

The toughest bunch of Rebels that ever lost a war, they fought for the South, and then for Texas, as the legendary Floating Outfit of "Ole Devil" Hardin's O.D. Connected ranch.

MARK COUNTER was the best-dressed man in the West: always dressed fit-to-kill. **BELLE BOYD** was as deadly as she was beautiful, with a "Manhattan" model Colt tucked under her long skirts. **THE YSABEL KID** was Comanche fast and Texas tough. And the most famous of them all was **DUSTY FOG**, the ex-cavalryman known as the Rio Hondo Gun Wizard.

J. T. Edson has captured all the excitement and adventure of the raw frontier in this magnificent Western series. Turn the page for a complete list of Berkley Floating Outfit titles.

J. T. EDSON'S
FLOATING OUTFIT
WESTERN ADVENTURES
FROM BERKLEY

TRIGGER FAST

B®

BERKLEY BOOKS, NEW YORK

Originally published in Great Britain by Brown Watson Ltd.

This Berkley book contains the complete
text of the original edition.
It has been completely reset in a typeface
designed for easy reading, and was printed
from new film.

TRIGGER FAST

A Berkley Book / published by arrangement with
Transworld Publishers Ltd.

PRINTING HISTORY
Brown Watson edition published 1964
Corgi edition published 1969
Berkley edition / November 1983

ISBN: 0–425–06297–X

A BERKLEY BOOK® TM 757,375
Berkley Books are published by The Berkley Publishing Group,
200 Madison Avenue, New York, New York 10016.
The name "BERKLEY" and the stylized "B"
with design are trademarks belonging to
Berkley Publishing Corporation.
PRINTED IN THE UNITED STATES OF AMERICA

CHAPTER ONE

The Rosemary-Jo Lament

STANDING waist deep in the cool clear water of the swimming hole Freda Lasalle rubbed soap over her slender, naked young body. Overhead the sun, not yet at noonday height, gave forth enough warmth to make this outdoor bathing both pleasant and possible.

Only rarely these days did Freda, daughter of the ranch's owner and sole woman of the house since the death of her mother, have a chance to bathe and swim in such complete freedom. The two cowhands her father hired were poor spirited men who would be only too willing to hide and watch her bathe, drooling over the sight of her naked beauty. However, her father took the two men to town with him earlier that morning and she had the ranch to herself.

Freda did not intend to miss such a chance. She had cleaned out the kitchen stove as her first chore after breakfast and wanted to wash the soot and grime from her body. Until her father returned from Barlock with supplies she could do nothing about making a meal so she took the time to bathe, stripping off her clothes in the house and running naked to the water, then plunging in to splash happily around.

The girl made an attractive picture as she stood working the soap lather into her short brown hair, although the only witness appeared to be the redbone hound which lay on the bank and watched her. She stood almost five foot six, a slim, willowy girl in her late teens, blossoming forth into full womanhood. Her face had charm, without being out and out beautiful. It was a warm, friendly face, one a man would not easily forget. Given another couple of years her figure would fully ripen and as yet the Texas Panhandle weather had not

1

made her skin coarse or harshened the texture of her hair.

She looked at the small frame house with some pride, then
ducked her head under the water to rinse the soap from her
hair. The house might be small, but she kept it spotlessly clean
and neat. Between the stream and the house stood a small pole
corral, empty now, but large enough to hold the small remuda
and harness horses they owned. To one side of the house stood
a barn, stable and a couple more small wooden buildings, to
the rear was a chicken pen and beyond that a backhouse.

On the side of the river away from her home a bank rose
fairly steep in most places, but sloping down more gently to a
ford below the swimming hole. Beyond the bank, a mile away,
lay the two mile wide strip along which, by convention, the
cattle herds stuck as they trailed north by the Lasalle place to
the Kansas railheads. The passing herds caused little trouble
and, as yet, the first of the new season had not come up from
southern Texas.

Ever since her father came home from a Yankee prisoner-
of-war camp, a sick man whose doctor warned he must get out
into the dry plains country or die, this small ranch had been
Freda's home. In the early days their neighbours helped them
build the house, showed Lasalle much he needed to know,
joined in with such communal tasks as gathering the free-
grazing herds of cattle and cutting out each other's stock. The
great trail drives wending their way north proved to be a boon
to the small ranchers in this section. To the trail bosses they
sold their surplus stocks, thus saving the expense of shipping
the cattle north to market. True they might have made more
money in Kansas, but the long drive north would eat that same
money up, even if a small outfit handling maybe a couple of
hundred head could have got through alone. Often too the
trail bosses would turn over unwanted calves born on the way
north and in that way helped bring new blood to the range.

In many ways it had been a lonely life for Freda, especially
since her mother died. She grew up in healthy surroundings,
free as a bird. Before her mother died she rode the range like a
man, she could handle a horse, use a shotgun well enough and
also could cook, mend or make clothes, do the chores a
woman in a lonely ranch was expected to do.

Now she wondered how long the happy life might continue.
To the north and west ran the great Double K ranch, the Lindon Land Grant, one of the huge open-range outfits for which

Texas had long been famous. When Lindon owned and ran it the Double K took its share in the local round-ups, helping out the smaller and less fortunate folk. Then old man Lindon died and his sole kin, back east, sold out the holding to an Englishman called Sir James Keller. At least so rumour had it for nobody had seen the mysterious new owner.

They felt his presence though. Two days before Brent Mallick, the local Land Agent and attorney for the Double K, paid a visit to Lasalle's and offered to buy them out. Freda remembered how Mallick smiled when her father refused the offer. There had been neither amusement nor friendship in the smile, nor on the faces of the two tough looking men who accompanied Mallick. She shuddered as she thought of Mallick's smile, with its implied threat—

> "A Yankee rode into West Texas,
> A mean kind of cuss and real sly,
> He fell in love with sweet Rosemary-Jo,
> Then turned and told her goodbye."

The redbone hound came to his feet even before Freda heard the pleasant tenor voice singing an old cowhand song. She threw a startled glance to where the bank of the stream hid the singer from view. From the sound of his voice he must be coming straight towards the house.

> "So Rosemary-Jo told her tough pappy,
> Who said, 'Why *hombre* that's bad,
> In tears you done left my Rosemary-Jo,
> No Yankee can make my gal sad.' "

The second verse of the Rosemary-Jo Lament came as Freda hurriedly waded out of the water. She grabbed up the towel from the shore and then ran for the house, the redbone following and helping scatter the chickens which scratched and pecked before the house.

> "He whipped out his two trusty hawg-legs,
> At which he warn't never slow,
> When that Yankee done saw them a-spitting,
> He said, 'It is time for to go!' "

                    *   *   *

Even as Freda reached the house and dashed inside, slamming the door behind her, she heard another verse of the song. The windows of the room stood open and as she could hear the singer clearly, she knew he must be close. She could hear the sound of more than one horse's hooves.

> "He jumped on his fast running pinto,
> Lit out like hell for the west,
> When Rosemary-Jo got her a fortune,
> He come back and said, 'I love you best.' "

Still drying herself Freda went to where she could peer out of a window and see the top of the river bank. Three riders came into sight, halting their horses at the head of the slope. Three cowhands from their dress, each astride a big, fine looking horse. The singer led a packpony which looked to be carrying their warbags and bed-rolls.

> " 'No no' cried she in a minute,
> 'I love me a Texan so sweet,
> And I'm going down to San Antone town,
> My sweet, loving Texan to meet.' "

The singer lounged in his saddle at the left of the party. Sitting his huge white stallion with easy grace, there appeared to be something wild, almost alien about him. His black, low-crowned, wide-brimmed Stetson hat thrust back from curly hair so black it almost shone blue in the light and the face it framed looked to be Indian dark, very handsome, babyishly innocent and young. From hat, down through tight rolled bandana, shirt, gunbelt, levis trousers, to boots he wore but one colour, black. The blackness was relieved only by the white, ivory she guessed, hilt of the bowie knife at his left side and the walnut grips of the old Colt Dragoon revolver hanging at his right.

The young rider's white horse moved restlessly, allowing her to see the low horned, double girthed Texas rig. That went without saying, a man who dressed in such a manner would use that kind of saddle. She also saw the butt of a rifle under the rider's left leg.

* * *

"So the Yankee went to the back country,
He met an old pal, Bandy Parr,
Who captained the Davis' State Police,
And a meeting they held in the bar."

They did not appear to be in any hurry, she thought, finishing drying herself and grabbing up clothing. The rider at the right side took her attention next for she could never recollect seeing a finer figure of a man. He towered over the other two, three inches at least over the six-foot level. For all his great size, the width of his shoulders, the tapering to a slim waist, he sat his seventeen hand bloodbay stallion with easy grace. He looked to be a light rider, the sort of man who took less out of his mount than a smaller, though less skillful person.

His costly white Stetson carried a silver concha decorated band, was on the same pattern as the other two's. It set on a head of golden blond hair, shading a face which had a classic, handsome cast of feature like those of a Greek god of old. His tan shirt had clearly been made to his measure, the bandana around his throat looked to be pure silk. In his dress he seemed to be something of a dandy, yet he also looked remarkably competent and those matched, ivory butted Army Colts in his holsters did not look like decorations, but hung just right for fast withdrawal.

"Rosemary-Jo got word to her pappy,
He fogged on his strawberry roan,
And said, 'From that ornery critter,
I'll save Rosemary who's my own.' "

By now Freda was struggling into her dress. Her head popped out of the neck like a squirrel peeping from its den-hole in a sycamore tree. She looked at the center man of the trio. She gave him barely more than a glance for, compared with his friends, he faded into nothing.

He didn't look tall like the other two, being at least six inches under the wiry six-foot length of the black-dressed, baby-faced boy. If his clothes were of as good quality as those worn by the others he did not have the flair to show them off so well. A costly black Stetson sat on his dusty blond hair. The face under the hat seemed to be handsome, though not as eye-catching as that of either of his friends. His shoulders had a width and appeared to be sturdy enough, but he faded into nothing compared with the giant build of the big blond. Even the brace of white handled 1860 Army Colts which rode butt forwards in his holsters did nothing to make him more noticeable. Freda smiled as she glanced at the gunbelt. The small, insignificant cowhand must badly want everyone to think of him as a real hard *hombre* and tried to improve the impression by going armed in the same manner as his friend.

> "Now the Yankee went down to San Antone,
> Met the Texas boy out on the square,
> But his draw was too slow, and as far as I know,
> That Yankee's still lying out there."

With the final verse of the song ended the three men rode slowly down the slope. At that moment, for the first time, Freda realized her position, alone in the house and far from any help. Three strangers, gun-hung and handy looking, came riding down towards her. They could be hired hard-cases from Double K for by now all the old cowhands of the spread were gone, being replaced by men whose ability with guns exceeded their skill with cattle.

Freda turned from the window and headed to collect the shotgun which hung with a Le Mat carbine, over the fireplace. She took down the ten gauge, two barrelled gun, checked the percussion caps sat on their nipples and then stood uncertain as to what her next move should be.

"Hello the house!" called a voice from outside. "Can we ride through the water?"

Which did not seem like the action of a hard-case bunch coming to scare her father into selling the ranch. The girl realized she might be doing her callers less than justice with her suspicions. She crossed the room, leaned the shotgun by the door, opened it and stepped on to the small porch.

"Come ahead," she called.

The Lasalle family might be poor, but they still offered hospitality to any passing stranger.

Slowly the big paint stallion, ridden by the smallest man, moved into the water, followed by the white, bloodbay and pack horse. Freda studied the horse, seeing it to be as fine looking and sizeable as either of his friends' mounts. It didn't look like the kind of horse one would expect so small and insignificant a man to be afork. Probably it belonged to that handsome blond giant and he allowed the small cowhand to ride it. Yet at that the small man must be better than fair with horses for the paint stallion did not look like the kind of animal to accept a man on it unless the man be its master.

Just as the men came ashore Freda felt something was wrong. Then she realized what. She had not fastened her dress up the back! The men were ashore now and she needed to think fast, to gain time to make the necessary adjustments. A flash of inspiration came to her.

"Take the horses around back," she told the three men. "Let them graze while you come in for a meal."

Not until the three men rode around the house and out of sight did Freda move. Then she stepped back into the house and began to fumble with the dress fastenings. At the same moment she realized that apart from a few eggs the ranch could offer its guests nothing by way of food.

The front of the house consisted of one big room, serving as both dining and sitting room. The kitchen and three small bedrooms all opened off the front room, a handy arrangement from the girl's point of view. She entered the kitchen, saw the coffeepot stood ready and looked to her skillet ready to fry eggs. Through the window she saw her guests removing the saddles from their horses.

Freda opened the kitchen door and stepped out, getting her first close-up look of the three men. The blond giant looked even more handsome close up and Freda wished she had donned her best dress instead of this old working gingham. She hardly gave the small man a glance, although his face did seem older and more mature. The dark boy seemed even younger now he was in close. His face looked innocent—until one looked at the eyes. They were red hazel in colour, wild, reckless, savage eyes. They were not the eyes for such an innocent face. If the youngster was, as she had thought at first glance, only sixteen they had been sixteen dangerous and hard-living years to give him such eyes.

"Howdy ma'am," greeted the small man, removing his hat as he saw her and showing he had some strength in his small frame for he held the heavy double girthed saddle in his left hand. "Thank you kindly for the offer."

"Sure is kind, ma'am," agreed the giant, his voice also a

Texas drawl, but deep and cultured. "Our cooking's not what it used to be."

"And never has been," grinned the dark boy, looking even younger and more innocent as he swept off the Stetson hat.

Watching the men walk towards her Freda wished she had taken time out to put on a pair of shoes and tidy her hair which still fluffed out and showed signs of washing. Yet there had been time for none of it and she must make do as she was.

Each man laid his saddle carefully on its side clear of the door, by the wall of the house. No cowhand worth his salt ever rested his saddle on its skirts, or placed it where clumsy feet might step on it. A cowhand took care of his saddle for without it he could not work.

"Go on through and sit a spell," she told them, indicating the door into the front room. "I'll fetch in the coffee."

By the time Freda arrived with the coffee she found her guests sitting at the table, their hats hanging by the storm straps on the back of the chairs. Her eyes studied them, knowing them to be strangers to this part of the range.

"You're from down south, aren't you?" she asked, pouring the coffee into cups.

Under the rules of rangeland etiquette the host could ask that much without giving offence. It left the guests free to tell as much or as little as they wished.

"I didn't think it showed," drawled the dark boy.

"You aren't looking for work hereabouts?" she went on, hoping they were not. Such men would stiffen any fighting force and they would be powerful backing if they aimed to ride for Double K.

"Work, ma'am?" asked the blond giant. "The word near on scares us off our food."

"I tell you, ma'am," the small man went on. "In all the years I've known this pair I haven't once got them to do a hand-stroke of work."

Freda could hardly restrain a smile as she noted the way the small man spoke. He really must be wanting to impress her, make her believe he gave the other two orders, or was in a position to have to put them to work. Then she thought of the big paint stallion, a real valuable animal. The small man must be the son of a rich ranch owner and the other two hired to be his bodyguard. Yet neither of the tall men looked like the sort to take pay for being a wet-nurse.

The small man's eyes flickered around the room. It looked neat, clean, tidy without being so fussy a man wouldn't dare breathe in case he messed something up. None of the furniture looked new, but it had been well kept and expensive when new. The drapes at the window were clean and colourful, and enlivened the atmosphere. Over the fireplace hung a Le Mat carbine, one of the old type known as the "grapeshot gun". The upper of the twin, superposed barrels took the nine .42 balls in the chamber. The lower barrel had no rifling and threw out either a .50 calibre grapeshot, or a charge of buck-shot when needed.

Despite its brilliant conception the Le Mat was a weapon long out of date, yet the house showed no more modern wea-pons—except for the shotgun leaning by the door.

Following the small man's gaze, Freda gulped as she saw the gun. Nobody would keep a shotgun in such a position as a normal thing. Her eyes went back to the small man once more.

"Menfolks not at home?" he asked.

"Not just now," she replied, then went on hurriedly. "They'll be back any time now."

"Huh huh!"

He left it at that. The girl shut her mouth, holding down a remark about the men her father hired, one much more com-plimentary than they deserved. Some instinct told Freda she need not fear her guests even though she was alone.

The small man's eyes were on her face; they were grey eyes and met a gaze without flinching. Nor was there any of the slobbering stare of her father's hands in the way he looked at her. His eyes did not try to strip her clothes away and feast on her young body. He looked like a man with close women kin. He also looked in a manner which told Freda her last words had not fooled him one little bit.

Suddenly she became aware of the strength in the small man's face. She knew her first impression could have been wrong; there might be much more than was at first apparent about this small South Texas man. Her eyes dropped to his gunbelt, seeing the fine workmanship in it—and how well worn and cared-for it looked. He had none of the habits of a show-off, nor did he in any way, by voice or gesture, call attention to the fact that he wore two guns like a real bad *hombre*.

"I'm afraid we're clean out of everything but eggs," she

said, wanting to prevent her confusion showing.

"Lon," drawled the big blond, "you've got a head like a
hollow tree. What about those pronghorn steaks in the pack?"

"Ain't your fault we done got 'em, any old ways," replied
the dark boy who then turned to Freda. "There I was, ma'am,
trying to sneak up on that lil ole rascal. Then this pair
comes—"

"How about you-all sneaking through the door, sneaking to
the pack, sneaking out the steaks, then sneaking back and giving them to the lady," put in the small man. "You being so
sneaky and all."

Freda noticed the way the small man addressed his friend.
He spoke like a man long used to giving orders and having
them obeyed. The black dressed boy came to his feet and per-
formed the remarkable feat of draining his coffee cup while
bowing gracefully to her.

"Reckon I'll have to apologize for this pair, ma'am," he
said. "I can't take them no place twice. Folks won't even have
them back to apologize for the first time."

He replaced the cup on the saucer and headed out through
the kitchen. Freda followed and in a few minutes he returned
carrying a burlap sack and several thick antelope steaks
wrapped Indian-style in leaves.

"You-all take the thickest for yourself, ma'am," he told
her. "We're riding greasy-sack, so take whatever you need out
of the bag."

The girl understood his meaning. To ride greasy-sack meant
that they had no chuckwagon along and so carried their food
in a burlap bag. She opened the bag to find it contained
potatoes, carrots, onions and a few cans of tomatoes, corn
and peaches.

Since the arrival of the three men Bugle, the redbone hound,
had stuck pretty close to his mistress, showing no sign of
friendship, following her into the kitchen. Now his tail wagged
as he caught the scent of fresh meat.

"You come friendly all of a sudden," drawled the dark boy.
"Is it me or this here meat you're in love with?"

"I can't take your food!" Freda gasped.

"Don't let that worry you, ma'am," he replied, tossing a
two pound steak to the waiting jaws of the redbone. "Too
much food makes Mark 'n' Dusty get all mean and ornery.
Only with Dusty, him being the boss, you can't most times tell

no difference. Say, was it all right for me to feed your dawg, ma'am?''

Freda nodded. She thought she had the three men sorted out now. The dark boy's name appeared to be Lon and from what he just said about Dusty being the boss it ought to make the small man's name Mark, for he was not likely to be the other two's employer.

At that moment the small man came to the kitchen door.

"Whatever Lon's telling you, ma'am," he said, "it's likely to be all lies."

"Just telling the lady what a sweet, kind 'n' loving nature you-all got, Dusty," Lon replied. "Course, like you said, it's all lies."

The words puzzled Freda more than ever. The small man's name appeared to be Dusty and that made him the boss. Then she thought she had the solution, Dusty was their boss' son and they treated him in such a manner as a result of it.

"You wouldn't be looking for the Double K, would you?" she asked.

"Double K?" Dusty replied. "That's the old Lindon Land Grant, isn't it?"

"It was. Lindon died and an Englishman bought it."

"We've never been this way before, have we, Lon?" drawled the small man. "I run my herds over the eastern trails, it's better for us that way."

Once more Freda noticed how he spoke; as if he was the trail boss when his ranch sent a herd to market. Yet he did not seem to speak in a boasting manner, or to be trying to impress her.

Through her cooking and the meal which followed Freda tried to understand the man called Dusty. The other two regarded him as their boss. Yet, from the banter which flowed between them, they were also good friends with much in common.

"You mean you came along the stream?"

The words came in a gasp from Freda as the import of something Mark just said sank into her puzzled head. A blush came to her cheeks for if they had been riding the bank of the stream they must have seen her bathing.

"Why else do you reckon we'd put up with Lon's caterwauling?" asked Dusty, a smile on his lips. It was a friendly smile, not the leer of a venal sneak who would sit watching a nude girl in the privacy of her bathing.

Then Freda understood and the blush died away. The three men must have spotted her from a fair way back down the river. To avoid causing her any embarrassment they swung from the bank edge and rode parallel to it but well clear, with Lon singing to warn her of their presence. They also took their time, allowing her a chance to get to the house and dress before riding in.

Tactfully, and in a diplomatic manner, Dusty swung the conversation away from the subject. Then Lon started her laughing with an exaggerated story of how he hunted and shot the pronghorn, which had tasted so delicious, despite having his two friends along.

The meal had ended but Freda wanted her guests to stay on and talk. She felt starved for company and good conversation and for the first time realized how lonely her life was.

Suddenly Bugle raised his head, looking across the room from where he had laid since finishing his steak. At the same moment Lon's youth and levity fell from him like a discarded cloak. He looked older, more alert—and deadly dangerous.

"Your pappy run seven—eight men, Miss Freda?" he asked.

"No, why?"

"There's that many coming up right now."

Then the others heard the sound of approaching hooves, coming at a good pace towards the river bank, down it and through the water. This had a special significance. The stream marked the boundary of the ranch house and nobody but the owners and their hired help had the right to cross without first calling for permission to do so.

Freda rose to her feet and darted to the door, opening it and stepping out. Eight men came across the stream, riding towards the house and halting their horses in a rough half-circle. They looked a hard bunch, with guns hanging low at their sides. She only knew one of the eight but could guess at the purpose of their visit.

The man she knew was called Preacher Tring—he'd been at Mallick's left hand when the Land Agent offered to buy them out. Now it looked as if Tring had returned to make sure the Lasalle family did sell out.

CHAPTER TWO

The Name's Dusty Fog

FREDA stepped across the porch and halted at the edge of it looking towards the eight men, not liking what she read in their eyes. They, with one exception, were men in the thirties or early forties, and with one exception wore cowhand dress—but they weren't cowhands.

Preacher Tring sat in the center of the group. A big blocky man with heavy rounded shoulders and a nose hooked like a buzzard's beak. He wore a round topped hat of the style circuit-riding preachers favored. His white shirt looked dirty, the black tie crooked. His sober black suit also looked stained and rumpled as if he'd worked hard in it that day. Around his waist hung a gunbelt, a brace of Navy Colts riding the fast draw holsters. Slouching in the saddle of a fine black horse Preacher Tring looked like a particularly evil buzzard perched ready to slash the eyes out of a corpse.

"What do you want?" Freda asked.

"We've come to move you folks on," answered Tring, his voice a harsh croak which was well suited to his looks. "Boss made you a good offer for this place. Now he allows you've had time to think about it. Price still goes, even after the place gets wrecked."

"How do you mean, wrecked?"

"Going to wreck the place, gal," Tring answered, waving a hand towards the buildings, then down to the corral. "Then happen your father doesn't sell out it won't just be the place we wreck."

Freda grabbed Bugle's collar as the dog stood by her side, his back hair rising and a low growl rumbling from his throat. She knew the men would shoot down her dog without a second thought and did not want that to happen.

"You wouldn't dare!" she gasped.

Without even troubling to reply Tring turned his horse and rode towards the corral. He unshipped the rope from his saddlehorn, tossed the noose over the right side gate post and secured the other end to the horn. Turning his horse he rode forward slowly until the rope drew taut. The big black threw its weight forward to try and drag whatever lay behind it.

Laughing and making coarse comments the men sat their horses and watched Tring. They did not trouble to look at the house, knowing the quality of Lasalle's hired hands and expecting no opposition except maybe from the rancher himself. Only Lasalle could not be at home or he would be outside and facing them.

"Go on, Preacher!" yelled the youngest of the bunch, a brash, tall youngster in his late teens and who clearly considered himself the hardest rock ever quarried. "Get off and push!"

This brought a roar of laughter from the others and a snarled curse from Tring. He often boasted of his horse's strength and pulling power, so did not intend to allow the animal to make him a liar.

Tring spurred his horse cruelly. Steel shod hooves churned up dirt as it threw weight against the taut rope, trying to tear the corral's post from the earth. The man cursed savagely as the post held firm. He raked his struggling horse from neck to rump with sharp-rowelled petmakers, but to no avail.

From behind Freda came the crash of a shot. The rope split and the horse, suddenly relieved of the strain, stumbled forwards, throwing its rider over its head. Tring's companions turned to see who dared interfere with the Double K.

The small Texan stood in the doorway of the house, smoke rising lazily from the barrel of the Army Colt in his right hand. He looked at the hostile group of eight hard-case riders.

"I'm taking cards," he said. "The name's Dusty Fog."

With that the sleek Colt pinwheeled on his finger and went back to the holster at the left side of his body. He stepped forward, passing the girl, to halt between her and the men.

Only it was not a small, insignificant cowhand who passed her. Now he seemed to have put on inches, and to exude a deadly menace. Never again would Freda think of him as being small.

He faced the men, hands thumb-hooked into his belt, eyes watching them, daring any of them to make a move.

Snarling out incoherent curses Preacher Tring sat up. He had lost his hat and his head was completely bald, which added to his general air of evil. He forced himself to his feet and looked at the small Texan. From the expression on Tring's face, Freda thought he would grab out his gun and shoot down this impudent stranger who came between him and his desires. In the heat of the moment Freda clean forgot about the other two men and did not wonder why they failed to stand alongside their boss at such a moment.

"Easy Preacher!" a man spoke hurriedly, urgently. "He's speaking true. That there's Dusty Fog all right. I saw him when he brought the Rocking H herd to Dodge against Wyatt Earp's word."*

Not until then did Freda fully realize who her small guest really was. She could hardly believe her eyes or ears as she looked at the small Texan called Dusty Fog.

She'd heard the name often enough, but never pictured the famous Dusty Fog as anything but a handsome giant, a hero of the same kind she read about in books. In the War Between The States she, and almost every other southern girl, dreamed of Dusty Fog as their knight in armor. He had been the boy-wonder, the Confederate Cavalry captain who, at seventeen, made the Yankees wish they'd stayed at home and who carried a fighting cavalryman's reputation as high as that of Turner Ashby or John Singleton Mosby.

Since the War his name rose high as a cowhand, a trail boss who ranked with Charlie Goodnight, Oliver Loving, Stone Hart, the pick of the trail bosses. It had been Dusty Fog and his friends who tamed the bad Montana mining city called Quiet Town,† after three lesser men died in the trying. He was the segundo of the great OD Connected ranch in the Rio Hondo country. He had ambidextrous prowess with his matched bone handled guns. His speed of drawing those same guns and his accuracy in shooting were all legends. Now he

* Told in TRAIL BOSS
† Told in QUIET TOWN

stood before Freda Lasalle, a man of five foot six at most, a man she had dismissed as nobody and hardly spared a second glance.

Tring also thought of all he had heard of Dusty Fog and liked none of it. The small Texan stood alone, facing eight of them—or did he stand alone—where he was two other men were likely to be.

The tall, handsome blond stood at the corner of the house. He stood with empty hands but that meant little for rumour had it that Mark Counter could draw and throw lead almost as fast as Dusty Fog. In his own right that handsome blond giant had a name himself.

If anything Mark's reputation as a cowhand stood higher than Dusty's. He had a name for being somewhat of a range country Beau Brummel who helped set cowhand fashions now as he had once done amongst the bloods of the Southern army. A rich man in his own right, son of a prosperous Big Bend rancher, Mark still rode as a hand for the OD Connected, working as a member of the floating outfit and siding Dusty in any trouble to come along. His strength was a legend, his skill in a rough-house brawl spoken of with awe and admiration wherever it was seen. How fast he could handle his gun was not so well known. He rode in the shadow of the Rio Hondo gun wizard for all that he stood a good six feet three inches tall.

Small wonder the hired guns from Double K looked uneasy when they saw Mark Counter all set to back his *amigo* against them.

Slowly Tring lowered the hands which had hung like curved talons over the butts of his Navy Colts. He'd been set to chance taking Dusty Fog with odds of eight to one in his favor. Eight to two were far from being bad odds, even eight to two those two—then the odds dropped to a level where Tring did not intend bucking against them.

A sinister double click announced another man stood at the side of the house opposite Mark Counter. Not one of the assembled gunhands thought it to be a trick of their ears, or imagination. That showed in the way they looked towards the dark boy, noting the twin barrel ten gauge in his hands.

Freda also looked and felt surprise. This was not the innocent looking boy who talked and joked with her inside the house. The clothes might be the same, but the face was a mean, cold, slit-eyed Comanche Dog Soldier's mask, alert, wolf-cautious and watching every move.

They called him Loncey Dalton Ysabel, the Ysabel Kid, *Cabrito* depending on how well folks knew him. Three names, but they all added up to one thing—a real dangerous *man*. His father had been a wild Irish-Kentuckian border smuggler, his mother the daughter of Chief Long Walker of the Comanche and his French-Creole squaw. That marriage brought a mixing of bloods which produced a deadly efficient fighting man with an innocent face and a power of danger inside him. He had the sighting eye of a backwoodsman of the legendary past and the same ability to handle a rifle. He could use his Dragoon Colt well enough when needed. From his French-Creole strain he gained an inborn love of cold steel as a weapon and an ability to use that James Black bowie knife which would not have shamed old Jim Bowie himself. Tied in with that came the skill of a Comanche Dog Soldier at riding anything with hair, ability to follow tracks where a buck Apache might falter and the keen eyes which came in so useful when riding scout. He could move through thick brush as silent as a shadow, speak seven languages and fluent Spanish. All in all it made the Kid a real good friend—or right bad enemy.

From the way he stood and watched the Double K men he was no friend.

"Don't see how all this comes to be your concern, Cap'n Fog," Tring said, in a much milder tone than he usually adopted. "These here nesters—"

"Stop handing us that bull-droppings, *hombre*!" growled Mark Counter, moving forward to flank Dusty and face the men. "These folk don't plough. They run a brand and keep cattle. That makes them ranch folks."

The youngster in Tring's bunch thought he was real fast with a gun. He had come through a couple of cowhand backing-down sessions and didn't reckon this trio would prove harder to handle than the others.

He swung down from his saddle to step by Tring and face the two Texans in his toughest and most belligerent manner, even though he wasn't showing good sense.

"Who asked you to bill in?" he asked in a tough voice.

"We're in, boy," Dusty answered, sparing him hardly a glance. "You, *hombre*, get afork your hoss and take your pards off with you."

Tring wasn't fixing to argue. He bent and took up his hat, placing it on the bald head. Tomorrow would be another day. The Texans would be riding on soon and he would return. Freda Lasalle was going to wish he had not when he came back. Or maybe Lasalle would pull out in a hurry when he heard what had happened—or what might have happened had not those three interfering Texans been on hand.

So Tring turned to collect his horse. His backers did not want trouble, he could read that on their faces. Only the fool kid wanted to make fuss, bring off a grandstand play.

Full of brash conceit and over-confident both in himself and the ability of the others to back him, the young hard-case took a pace forward.

"Listen, you!" he said to Dusty. "Our boss sent us to do a job, and we aim to do it, so you can smoke off afore you get hurt."

Dusty did not even look at the young man, but threw a glance at Tring as the bald man mounted his horse.

"Call him off, *hombre*," Dusty said gently, "or lose him."

Tring made no reply. He watched the young gun-hand, wondering if he might be lucky and give the rest of them a chance to cut in.

"Listen, you short-growed ru—!" began the youngster.

He stopped faster than he started, and without finishing his speech, for a very good reason. Dusty Fog glided forward a step. His right fist drove out and sank with the power of a mule-kick into the youngster's stomach. The young gunny's hand started moving towards the butt of his Army Colt as Dusty stepped forward. He failed to make it. The hand which he meant to fetch out the Colt clutched instead at his middle as he doubed over croaking in agony.

Instantly Dusty threw up his fist-knotted left hand, smashing it full under the youngster's jaw, lifting him erect and throwing him backwards into the horses. Then the gunny slid down into a sitting position. Through the spinning pain mists and bright lights which popped before his eyes he saw Dusty standing before him and again tried to get out his gun. Dusty jumped forward, foot lashing out in a kick which ripped skin from the gun-hand, brought a howl of pain from the youngster and sent the Colt flying.

Bending forward Dusty took a double handful of the youngster's shirt and hauled him erect, shook him savagely, then let him go. The youngster's legs were buckling under him as Dusty's right fist lashed up at his jaw. Mark Counter winced in sympathy as the blow landed. The youngster went over backwards, crashing down and made no attempt to rise.

Dusty looked at Tring, his eyes cold and hard.

"You always let a boy do your fighting?" he asked.

"Boy played it on his own," snarled Tring, hating backing down but not having the guts to take Dusty up on it. "We ain't after fuss with you."

"Fussing with a gal'd be more your game," drawled Mark. "Wouldn't it?"

Never the most amiable of men, Tring still managed to hold down his anger and resentment at Mark's words.

"The boss made these folks a fair offer for their place," he said. "He wants more land to build up his holding. We just figured to toss a scare into the girl and her pappy. Didn't mean her no real harm."

Freda watched everything, still holding Bugle's collar. She wanted to say something, take a part in the drama being played out before her. Dusty did not give her a chance for he clearly aimed to handle the entire affair his own way. She went back to shove Bugle into the house then came towards Dusty.

"We aren't selling," she said.

"You hear that?" asked Dusty.

"I heard it!" Tring replied.

"We'll be going up the trail today. But we'll be coming back this way and if these folks aren't here and unharmed, *hombre*, you'd best be long gone or I'll nail your hide to the door. Understand?"

"I understand, Cap'n Fog."

"Then get that kid on his horse and ride out of here."

A growled order from Tring brought two men from their horses to help the groaning youngster to his feet then into his saddle. Freda watched them, seeing the conspicuous way they kept their hands clear of the guns at all times. This puzzled her for, from what she had heard, Double K hired tough hard-cases.

Under the right circumstances Tring's bunch might have been hard and tough. Yet every last one of the seven who were capable of thought knew they faced three men who were with but few peers in salty toughness and were more than capable of handling a fight with guns or bare hands.

So the Double K's hard-case bunch got their horses turned and headed off, leaving behind an undamaged house and a Colt Army revolver lying where the youngster let it fall.

Among the other men, thinking himself either hidden from view or unsuspected of being able to do any harm, the youngster leaned forward over the saddlehorn. The way he hung forward he looked like he was still too groggy to do anything, but his left hand drew the rifle from his saddleboot. They passed through the river and rode up the slope. This was his chance. Thirty yards or more separated him from the three Texans and the girl. It was a good range for rifle work and not one at which a man might make an easy hit with a fast drawn Colt. He could turn, make a fast shot at that small bond runt who whipped him. Then he and the rest of the boys could make a stand on the rim and cut the other two down.

The horse was almost at the top of the slope when he wheeled it around in a tight, fast turn and started to throw up the rifle. The move came as a surprise to the other Double K riders. It did not appear to be so much of a surprise to the people against which the move had been directed. The youngster saw that almost as soon as he turned the horse.

Always cautious, more so at such a moment, the Kid stayed right where he had been all the time and did not join Mark and Dusty before the house. After watching Dusty hand the hard-case youngster his needings, the Kid rested the barrels of the ten gauge on his shoulder although his right hand still gripped the butt, forefinger ready on the trigger and hammers still pulled back.

From his place the Kid saw the leaning over and might have passed it off as a dizzy spell caused by the whipping Dusty had handed out. Then the Kid noticed the stealthy withdrawal of a rifle and he waited for the next move.

"Dusty!" the Kid snapped, even as the youngster swung his horse around.

With men like the three Texans to see was to act. Neither Dusty nor Mark had seen the rifle drawn, but they were watching for the first treacherous move, ready to copper any bet the other men made.

At the Kid's word Dusty went sideways, knocking Freda from her feet, bringing her to the ground. She gave a startled yell, muffled for he stayed on top of her, shielding her with his body. The girl heard that flat slap of a bullet passing overhead, but the crack of the shot was drowned by the closer at hand roar of the shotgun.

Even as he yelled his warning the Kid brought the shotgun from his shoulder. Its foregrip slapped into his waiting left hand, the butt settled against his shoulder and he aimed, then touched off first the right, then left barrel. He expected the charge to spread at thirty yards and was not disappointed in it. He did feel disappointed when the men let out howls, including the youngster who jerked up in his saddle, screamed in pain, turned the horse and headed after his bunch as they shot over the bank top and went from sight, although their horses could be heard galloping off beyond the rim.

Freda managed to lift her face from the dirt and peer out by Dusty. She saw Mark kneeling at one side, holding his right hand Colt at arm's length, resting his wrist on his left palm and his left elbow on his raised left knee. Her eyes went to the other side of the stream. She could see no bodies, nor any sign of Tring and his men.

Holstering his gun Mark walked to her side, she saw him towering above her. He bent down, gripped Dusty by the waistbelt, and with no more apparent effort than if lifting a baby hoisted him clear of the girl. Then in the same casual manner Mark turned and tossed Dusty at the Kid who came forward muttering something under his breath and too low for Freda to catch—which in all probability was just as well. Ignoring the choice and lurid remarks made about himself, his morals, descendants and ancestors by his friends, Mark bent and held a hand toward Freda.

"If you throw me I'll scream," she warned.

"Ma'am," Mark replied, gallantly taking the hand and

helping her rise. "I never throw a real good looking young lady away."

By the time Freda stood up again she found the Kid and Dusty had untangled themselves and the Kid came forward bearing the ten gauge and showing a look of prime disgust at such an ineffective weapon.

"What the hell have you got in this fool gun?" he growled. "I reckon to be better'n that with a scatter."

"I charged it with birdshot. There's been a chicken-hawk after the hens and so I—"

"BIRDSHOT!" the Kid's voice rose a few shades. "No wonder I didn't bust their hides. Landsakes, gal, whyn't you pour in nine buckshot?"

"Because I didn't think I'd need it!" she answered hotly, the reaction at her narrow escape almost bringing tears.

"Easy gal, easy," said Dusty gently. "Lon's only joshing you. It's just his mean old Comanche way. They've gone and they won't be back."

"Not today," she agreed bitterly, thinking of the morrow and the visit it would surely bring.

"Nor any other day," Dusty promised. "We'll call in at the Double K and lay it plain before the new boss. If he makes fuss for you we'll make it for him on our way down trail."

CHAPTER THREE

Wire Across The Trail

IT took Freda a couple of minutes to catch control of her nerves again. She made it in the end, helped by the thought of how lucky she had been. Tring and his men might have done much worse than wreck the buildings and rip down the corral on finding her alone at the house. She thought thankfully of the unfastened dress, it caused her to request the three Texans take their horses around back and then come in for a meal. That gave her a chance to fasten the dress. It also kept the horses out of sight. Had Tring and his men seen three fine looking animals such as Dusty, Mark and the Kid's mounts out front they might have waited in the background until the visitors departed.

"Whyn't you call in the local law?" Mark asked.

"In Barlock?" she replied. "There'd be more chance of help in a ghost town."

"Well," Dusty drawled, "We'll ride in and see their boss. It might do some good for you."

"Riders coming in, Dusty," remarked the Kid, walking towards the side of the house with his hand hanging by the butt of the old Dragoon and the despised shotgun trailing at the other side. "Three of them, coming from back there a piece."

Freda ran towards the Kid, sudden fear in her heart. She reached the corner of the house at the same time he did, staring across the range to where three men rode towards them, following the wagon trail into town. She clutched at the Kid's right arm, holding it tight.

"Don't shoot, Lon," she gasped. "It's my father!"

"Wasn't fixing to shoot, so let off crushing my dainty lil

23

arm," he replied. "You-all near on as jumpy as those other pair."

"Something's wrong. I'm sure something's wrong," she went on.

"Won't get any righter until we know what it is," Dusty answered, coming to the girl's side.

None of the approaching trio rode real good horses. Two were youngish, cowhands; although not such cowhands as the OD Connected would hire. The third looked in his late forties, sat his horse with something of a cavalryman's stiff-backed grace. It showed even slumped up and dejected as he looked. His clothes were not new, but they were clean and neat—and he didn't wear a gun. The three Texans saw this latter point even before they noticed the rest. A man without a gun was something of a rarity anywhere west of the Mississippi and east of the Pacific Ocean.

Nearer the house the three men split up, the hands making for the door which led into the room they used as living quarters. The older man rode forward, halted his horse and swung down from his saddle. His face bore a strong family resemblance to Freda, now it was lined and looked exhausted, beaten, like the face of a man who has taken all he can and wants to call it quits.

He came forward, hardly looking at the three Texans, laid his hand on his daughter's arm and shook his head gently.

"We're licked, Freda," he said. "Mallick has taken over the two stores and won't let any of us small ranchers buy supplies unless we pay cash."

"But Matt Roylan has always known our credit is good," she answered.

"Yes, but the Double K has taken over Matt and Pop Billings' notes at the bank and will foreclose if they sell. I saw Mallick, he said we could have all the supplies needed and he'd take it out of the price he offered for our place."

"He can't pull a game like that!" Dusty said quietly stepping forward.

"He's done it," George Lasalle answered.

"And the local law stands for it?" Mark asked.

"Elben, he's town marshal, takes orders from the Double K and has men supplied to back him."

Never had Freda felt so completely helpless and so near to

tears. They must have supplies, food at least, to tide them over until the first drive came up trail and they could sell cattle to the trail boss. Then they would have enough money to straighten their account, as they had in previous years.

"Sloane sold out," her father went on. "I saw his wagon before Billings' store, taking on supplies. Mrs. Sloane was crying something awful."

Then for the first time he seemed to become aware that there were strangers, guests most likely, present. Instantly he shook the lethargy from him and became a courteous host.

"I'm sorry, gentleman," he said. "I shouldn't be troubling you with our worries. Have you fed our guests, Freda?"

"We had a good meal, sir," Dusty replied. "Your daughter's a fine cook."

At that moment the two hired hands emerged from their room carrying what looked like all their gear. Without a word they swung afork their horses and rode away, not even giving a backwards glance. Dusty watched them, thinking how he would not take their kind as cook's louse even, but most likely they were the best hands Lasalle could afford to hire. Now it looked like they were riding out.

"Where're they going, papa?" Freda asked.

"They quit. A couple of Double K men saw them in town and told them to get out while they could. I told them I couldn't afford to pay them but they said they were going anyway."

"But we can't manage the place without their help," Freda gasped. "You can't gather and hold the shipping cattle alone and we have to get a herd to sell so we can buy supplies."

"Never knew that ole hoss of mine so leg-weary as now, Dusty," Mark remarked in a casual tone.

"Ole Blackie's a mite settled down and ain't willing to go no place at all," drawled the Kid. "And it looks like this gent needs him a couple or so hands for a spell."

Lasalle and his daughter exchanged glances. He did not know who these three young men might be, but he knew full well what they were. They looked like tophands in any man's outfit, seventy-five-dollar-a-month men at least and he could not afford to pay for such talented workers.

"Happen Mr. Lasalle here can let us stay on a spell we'll have to get word up to Bent's Ford and warn Cousin Red not to wait his herd for us," Dusty remarked more to himself than the others. He turned to Lasalle. "Take it kind if you'd let us stay on and rest our horses. We'll work for our food and bed."

A gasp left Freda's lips. She could hardly believe her ears and felt like singing aloud in joy. After seeing the way Dusty, Mark and the Kid handled the eight Double K hard-cases and made them back off, she did not doubt but that the ranch would be safe in their hands.

"We haven't much food," she said, "but the way you told it none of you do much work either."

From the grins on three faces Freda knew she had said the right thing. Her reply showed them she had the right spirit and knew cowhand feelings. Her father did not take the same lighthearted view.

"Just a moment, Freda," he put in. "These gentlemen are welcome to stay over and rest their horses, but we won't expect them to work for their food."

"Why not?" asked Dusty. "The way this pair eat they need work, or they'll run to hawg-fat and be good for nothing when I get them back to home."

"But—but—!"

"Shucks, give it a whirl, sir," interrupted Dusty. "Mark here's good for heavy lifting which don't call for brains. Lon might not know a buffalo bull from a muley steer, but he's better than fair at toting wood for the cook."

"And how about you?" asked Freda. "What do you do?"

"As little as he can get away with," Mark answered.

The girl laughed and turned to her father. "Papa, this is Captain Dusty Fog, Mark Counter and the Ysabel Kid."

It took Lasalle a full minute to reconcile Dusty's appearance with his Civil War record, or his peacetime prominence. Then Lasalle saw the latent power of the small man, recognized it as an old soldier could always recognize a born leader of men. His daughter was not a victim of cowhand humor. This small man was really Dusty Fog. He still did not know what he could say or do for the best.

Then his daughter took the matter out of his hands, made a decision of her own and showed him that she was a child no more.

"I'll show you where the hands bunked," she said. "You

can move your gear in and then I'll find you some work."

"I'm beginning not to like this here job already," the Kid told Dusty in an audible whisper. "This gal sounds too much like you and I'm all for a day's work—providing it's spread out over three days."

With that the three cowhands started to follow Freda, leaving her father with his mouth hanging open, not knowing how things came to happen. Then he recalled a piece of news overheard in town, something which might interest the three cowhands.

"Mallick's started wiring off their range. He's already fenced off the narrows all the way along their two mile length from the badlands down to where they open out on to his range again. He doesn't allow any trail herds to cross the Double K."

"He's done what?"

Lasalle took a pace backwards before the concentrated fury in Dusty's Fog's voice as the small Texan turned back towards him. Mark and the Kid had turned also and they no longer smiled or looked friendly.

"Put wire across the trail, clear across the narrows. Says any trail herd which wants to make the market has to swing one way or the other round his range."

The girl looked from her father to the three cowhands. She knew cowhands hated barbed wire and fences of any kind. She knew all the range arguments about wire; that cattle ripped themselves open on the spikes; that a man might ride into such a fence during the night hours and not see it until too late. She also knew the hate went deeper than that. From the Mississippi to the Pacific a man could move or let his cattle graze without being fenced in. He could ride where he wished and had no need to fear crossing another man's land as long as he obeyed the unwritten rules of the range. Through all that expanse of land there were few if any fences and the free-roaming cowhands wanted to see it stay that way.

"How about the herds already moving north?" Mark asked quietly. "This's the trail Stone Hart uses and he's already on his way."

"I think we'd all better go into the house and talk this out," Lasalle replied, but some of the tired sag had left his shoulders now and he seemed to be in full command of himself.

He led the way around the house side and in through the front door. The Kid collected the fallen Army Colt, although Lasalle paid no attention to it, or to the shotgun which the Kid leaned against the door on entering. He waved his guests into chairs and rooted through the side-piece drawers to find a pencil and paper. With these he joined the others at the table and started to make a sketch map of the outline of the Double K. It looked like a rough square, except that up at the north-eastern corner the narrows thrust out to where it joined the badlands. All in all Lasalle drew quite a fair map, showing his own place, the other small ranches and the general lay of the land.

"Did some map-making with the Field Engineers during the War," he remarked. "This's the shape of the Lindon Land Grant. We ranch here. This was the Doane place, but they've sold out. This's the Jones place and the last one here is owned by Bill Gibbs. The town's back here, out beyond the Double K's south line. If the new owner can buy us out it will make his spread cover a full oblong instead of having the narrows up here."

Taking the pencil Dusty marked the line taken by the north-bound trail herds. He tapped the narrows with the pencil tip. Freda noticed that he handled the pencil with his left hand, yet he drew his Colt with his right. He must be truly ambidextrous, she thought.

"And he's run wire down this way," Dusty said. "From the badlands up that way, right down to where the river starts to curve around and down to form his south line."

"So I've heard. I haven't been out that way."

"Which means any drive that comes up is going to have to swing to the west," Mark drawled. "Or go east and try to run the badlands."

Lasalle nodded. "Mallick claims the trail herds won't cross Double K."

"Which'd mean the drive would have to circle right around their range to the west, lose maybe a week, maybe more's drive, or cut east and face bad water, poor graze, worse country and the chance of losing half the herd," said Mark quietly. "I can't see any trail boss worth his salt doing that."

"Me neither," agreed the Kid. "What do we do about it, Dusty?"

"Wait until the Wedge comes up and see what Stone allows to do."

"Huh!" grunted the Kid, for once not in agreement with Dusty's reply. "I say let's head up there to the narrows and haul down that fence."

"The Double K have twenty men at least on the spread," Lasalle put in. "They have such law as exists in this neck of the woods. Elben has eight men backing him in Barlock, all being paid by the Double K."

"Which sounds like a powerful piece of muscle for a man just aiming to run a peaceful cow outfit," drawled Dusty. "Have you seen this new owner?"

"Nobody has yet, apart from the hard-cases stopping folks crossing their range. They say the new owner hasn't arrived yet, that he bought the place without even seeing it."

"So we don't know if he is behind this wiring the range or not."

"No, Captain, we don't. Only it's not likely Mallick would be doing all this off his own shoulders is it? It'd take nearly four mile of barbed wire to make a double fence along the narrows and that runs to money."

Changing hands Dusty started to doodle idly on the paper. This ambidextrous prowess was something he had taught himself as a child, mainly to take attention from his lack of inches. He thought of Englishmen he had known, a few of them and not enough to form any opinion of such men as a whole. Yet none of those he had known ever struck him as being the sort to make trouble for folks who couldn't fight back.

"We ought to head over and see if this English *hombre's* to home, Dusty," growled the Kid, sounding Comanche-mean.

"It'll wait until we've a few more men," Dusty replied.

"Hell, after they come here today—"

Lasalle stared at the Kid. This had been the first time Tring's visit received a mention. Freda hurriedly told of the arrival of the Double K men, their threat to the property and their departure. The rancher's face lost some of its colour, then set in grim lines as he thought of what might have happened had Dusty, Mark and the Kid not been on hand. His attempts to thank the three young Texans met with no success for they laughed it off and, the way they told it, Freda did the running off wielding a broom to good effect on the hard-case crew.

All in all Dusty seemed far more interested in the closing of the trail than in being thanked for a very necessary piece of work.

"Lon," he said. "Reckon you could find Bent's Ford, happen you was looking for it?"

"Likely, but I'm not looking."

"You are. Just as soon as you've thrown a saddle on that white goat out back."

"Be late tonight when I get there," drawled the Kid.

"Happen that fool Blackie hoss makes it," grinned Mark.

"Ole Blackie'll run hide 'n' tallow off that brown wreck you ride," scoffed the Kid. "I'll make Bent's tonight all right, only I might find the hard boys have been here and took off with your guns."

"I'm here to protect them, Lon," Freda put in.

"Sure, with birdshot in both barrels. Say, reckon you can throw up a bite of food to eat on the way, something I can carry easy."

She sniffed. "I'll flavor it with birdshot. Just remember that I've nothing in the house, except for what's in your greasysack."

"Do what you can," Dusty suggested. "Then Mark and I'll take you into town and buy supplies."

"Mallick won't let us buy anything on credit," Lasalle pointed out.

"We never said anything about credit."

An indignant flush came to Lasalle's cheeks as he caught the meaning of Dusty's words. He thrust back his chair and came to his feet, facing the small Texan across the table.

"I can't accept charity—"

"And none's being offered. Man, you're the touchiest gent I've come across in many a year. This's a loan until Stone Hart arrives and you can sell some stock."

"And any way you look at it Dusty and I'm going to eat our fair share of that same food."

Freda stepped to her father's side and laid a hand on his sleeve, her fingers biting into the bicep.

"We accept," she said and her voice once more warned her

father not to argue. "Thank you all for helping."

"There's another thing though," Lasalle said, surrendering the field to his daughter. "Mallick has told the storekeepers they won't serve any small ranch folk unless they bring a note from him. He keeps a deputy in each store to make sure the owner obeys."

"Well now," drawled Mark idly, "reckon we could do something about that, don't you, Dusty?"

While agreeing with this big *amigo* on the point that they could do something about it, Dusty did not want to make war in Barlock until he had a fighting force at his back. While he and Mark could likely go into town and make Elben's deputies sing low, they might also have to do it to the tune of roaring guns and that could blow things apart at the seams. Dusty wished to avoid starting hostilities if he possibly could. It was not fear of odds which worried Dusty, odds could be whittled down and hired gunmen did not fight when the going got too stiff. With the Wedge at his elbow Dusty could make the hired hard-cases of Double K think the going had got too stiff, then likely put its new owner where he must make his peace.

Every instinct warned Dusty that more than lust for land lay behind this business. The Lindon Land Grant spread wide and large enough to satisfy a man, especially a man new to the cattle business. The entire area was well watered, that could not be the cause fo the trouble. So he must look deeper for the reason and when he found it would best know how to avert trouble.

Dusty wanted to meet the English owner if he could, Mallick certainly, to get the measure of his enemies, if enemies they should be. It might be that both were new to the west and did not know the cattleman's hatred of barbed wire, or the full implication of Lindon's Grant. If so, and they listened, he might be able to steer them in the right direction.

"What do you want me to do at Bent's, Dusty?" asked the Kid, breaking in on his pard's thought train.

"Leave word for Cousin Red to carry on up trail without us. I don't want him waiting at Bent's, or coming back to help us. That herd has to make the market. And don't spread the word about this wire trouble. I don't want this section swarming with hot-headed fools all looking for trouble."

"They'd likely be down here and rip down that fence," drawled the Kid. "Which same could sure show the Double K bunch how folks feel."

"And might start lead flying." Dusty answered.

He looked beyond the mere basic events. If Keller or Mallick aimed to keep the fence they had trained fighting men to help them. No matter what public opinion might think about the fences Keller had the law behind him in his right to erect one.

Before any more could be said Freda came in and announced she had food ready for the Kid's departure. So setting his black Stetson at the right "jack-deuce" angle over his off eye, the Kid headed out back to saddle his white stallion.

The girl followed him and watched the big white horse come to his whistle. She had the westerner's love of a good horse and that seventeen hand white stallion sure was a fine animal.

"Isn't he a beauty?" she said, stepping forward. "Can I stroke him?"

"Why sure," grinned the Kid, "happen you don't want to keep both hands. See, old Blackie here's mammy done got scared with a snapping turtle just afore he was born and he don't know whether he's hoss or alligator."

Freda studied the horse and decided that, despite the light way he spoke, the Kid called it right when he told of the dangerous nature of his horse. That seventeen-hand white devil looked as wild and mean as its master. So she refrained from either touching or approaching the horse. This was a real smart move for Blackie would accept the touch of few people, in fact only the Kid could handle his horse with impunity, it merely tolerated the other members of the floating outfit when circumstances forced them to handle it.

With his horse saddled ready to ride the Kid went astride in a lithe, Indian-like bound. He looked down at Freda and grinned, the grin made him look very young and innocent again. Removing his hat he gave her an elaborately graceful flourish with it, then replaced it.

"You get some buckshot in that gun, gal," he said, "and afore I get back here. *Birdshot,* huh!"

Before she could think up a suitable reply he turned the horse, rode around the side of the building, through the water and up the slope. He turned, waved a cheery hand, then went from sight.

Only then did she realize that he had not asked for directions to Bent's Ford. A momentary suspicion came to her for Dusty claimed they had never travelled this way before. Then the thought left her and she felt just a little ashamed of herself at having it. The Ysabel Kid needed no spoken directions to help him find his way across country. Out there, although the first drive of the year had not yet passed, he would find enough sign to aim him north and all the trails converged at Bent's Ford in the Indian Nations.

"Lon gone?" Dusty asked, coming to the front door as the girl returned to the house.

"No. He's sat on the roof, playing a guitar."

Somehow Freda felt in a mad gay mood, far happier than she had done for a long time. She gave a guilty start, realizing it must be the excitement of the day and the pleasure at having company which made her act in such a manner.

CHAPTER FOUR

A Pair of Drunken Irresponsible
Cowhands

"ABOUT these supplies?" Mark Counter asked as Dusty and Freda entered the room from seeing the Kid on his way to Bent's Ford.

"I've told, Mark," Lasalle replied. "Mallick won't let us buy any unless we sell out to him."

"Looks like we'll just have to go in and see Mr. Mallick," drawled Dusty.

"Poor Mallick," Freda remarked, the gay mood still on her.

Her father watched her and for the first time realized how lonely she must be out here miles from town. He wondered if they might be better to take Mallick's offer, leave the ranch and make a fresh home in a town where she could have friends of her own age.

Then he thought of the strength Mallick had in Barlock. With Elben, the town marshal, backed by eight gun-wise hard-case deputies, Dusty and Mark would be hopelessly out-numbered. They stood a better than fair chance of leaving town headed in a pinewood box for the boothill.

"It's risky—!" he began.

"Could be, happen we rode on in and started to shoot up the main drag," Dusty agreed. "Only we don't aim to. We'll just ride on in peaceable and ask him to act a mite more sociable and neighborly."

"And if he doesn't want to act more sociable and neigh-borly?" Freda asked.

"Don't reckon there's much we can do at all," drawled Mark, sounding mild but there was no mildness in his eyes.

" 'Cepting maybe try moral suasion," Dusty went on, just as mild sounding.

"Ole Dusty's real good at that, too," Mark said. "Yep. I can't think of a better moral suader than him. Excepting maybe his Uncle Devil and his cousin Betty."

"And what if Mallick doesn't fall for this moral suasion—whatever that might be?"

"Tell you, gal," Mark answered. "We'll likely hide behind you."

They left it at that, although Freda wondered what moral suasion might be. Her father was smiling now, looking more confident in himself all the time, more like the man she always remembered. Freda saw for the first time the strain he had been under for the past few years since her mother died. Now he looked better, ready to take on the world and its problems.

"Where at's your hosses, gal?" Mark asked, taking up his hat.

"Out back, grazing, I'll show you."

"I've seen a couple of hosses afore, gal, can likely tell them from a cow, happen the cow's not a muley. I'll hitch a hoss to your buggy for you."

Freda smiled. "I'll come along, there's a muley cow or two out back and I wouldn't want to drive into town behind it."

"Pick a couple of saddle horses out for us, Mark," Dusty put in. "No sense in going in there shouting who we are."

"Yo!"

With the old cavalry reply Mark turned and left the room with Freda on his heels. Lasalle watched her go, then turned to Dusty with a worried look in his eyes.

"I've never seen Freda act that way," he said. "It's—well—."

"Yeah, I know," grinned Dusty. "I've seen girls get that way around Mark afore. Don't worry, it won't get serious and you can trust Mark." He nodded to the old Le Mat carbine on the wall. "Does that relic work?"

Indignant at the slur on his prized Le Mat, Lasalle forgot his daughter's infatuation for Mark Counter and headed to the wall. He lifted down the Le Mat and walked to the table.

"Work!" he snorted. "I'll say it works. And I'll show Tring just how well if he comes back today."

Dusty grinned. "Way him and his bunch took off," he

drawled, "they were toting birdshot and they won't feel like riding anyplace today."

With that he took up the young gunhand's discarded Army Colt. He turned the weapon in his hands, checking its chamber was full loaded and that the weapon worked. It had some dirt in it, but the Colt 1860 Army revolver was a sturdy weapon and took more than a bit of dirt to put it out of working condition. He rubbed the dirt off the revolver, set the hammer at half cock and turned the chamber, making sure it would rotate properly.

"Here, let me handle that," Lasalle said. "You said the Kid used the shotgun on Double K?"

"Both barrels and a good ounce of birdshot, way they took to hollering when it sprayed out," Dusty answered. "So shove in some powder and pour a load of buckshot on top this time. It doesn't fan out but it's a mite more potent close up."

Outside Mark caught the best two of the ranch's small bunch of saddle stock and led them back to the house. He slung his saddle blanket on one horse, then the double girthed range rig while Freda watched. He felt her eyes on him and hoped she wasn't going to get involved in romance that could have no successful end.

Mark did not mind a mild flirtation but he made a rule never to become involved with a sweet, innocent and naïve girl like Freda. In his travellings around the west he had seen, and known intimately, a number of women who were either famous already, or would be one day. They were all mature women who knew what time of day it was and knew better than to expect anything permanent to come of romance with a man like him.

For all his worries Mark did the girl less than justice. Freda did not think of herself as being halfway towards marrying him. Some woman's instinct warned her it would be no use falling in love with a man like Mark. Yet she wanted to be near him, to see how he walked and talked, so that she might know the feeling again if it came with a more marriageable man's presence.

She pointed out the harness horse and helped Mark hitch it to the small buckboard wagon. Then they walked back to the house to find her father sitting at the sitting-room table with a formidable collection of weapons before him.

"We're ready to go, Dusty," she said.

"Reckon you can hold down the house while we're gone, George?" Dusty asked her father.

"Can I?" growled Lasalle. "I reckon with old Bugle here to give warning and all this artillery I just might be able to."

"Keep the shotgun handy then. It's got buckshot down the barrels—I saw to that."

Freda poked her tongue out at Dusty and headed for the door. He grinned, took up his hat and followed her out. Lasalle came to the kitchen door, the Le Mat carbine resting on his arm and the Army Colt thrust into his waistband. Freda could see the change in her father now. He looked almost as young and happy as he had on his leaves during the war, before being taken prisoner and sent to a Yankee hell-hole prisoner-of-war camp.

At first Freda kept up a light-hearted flow of banter with the two men as they rode by her on borrowed horses. They kept to the wheel-rut track the buckboard carved into the ground on many trips to Barlock, travelling across good range country with water, grass and a good few head of long-horn cattle grazing in sight of them. Freda saw the way Dusty and Mark watched the range, studying it with keen and careful eyes, watching for some sign of approaching danger, even while they laughed and joked with her.

Not until they were halfway to town did Freda mention the trouble.

"Why did you stay on to help us, Dusty?" she asked.

"It could be because I like you folks and don't take to Double K shoving you around," he replied.

"It wouldn't be because of that fence, too?"

"That's part of it," Dusty agreed. "The range has always been open and I'd hate to see it fenced. There's no need. A man's cattle can roam, feed anywhere the graze is good and not cut the grass down to its roots because they're hemmed in by a fence. Down home in the Rio Hondo our round-ups take a month and cover maybe three hundred square miles. We work with the other outfits, share the profits, take our cut. Any stock from out of our area is held until it's spread's rep. comes for it and we send men to collect ours."

"The fence blocks a cattle trail, Freda," Mark went on soberly. "Which makes it a whole lot worse. You didn't see

Texas right after the war. Not the way I saw it when I came though with Bushrod Sheldon on our way to join Maximillian. There were cattle every place a man looked and no market for them. Then we found a market up north and men started to move their herds up towards Kansas. It was the trail herd which saw this area opened up, the Indian moved on out. Men died on those early drives, more than do these days. They were learning the lessons we know now and a lot of times a man didn't get a chance to profit from a mistake. A code grew up, gal. The code of the trail boss, the way he and his crew lived on the trail. One thing no trail boss will do is risk losing his herd and that's what it'd mean to push 'round here.''

The girl watched Mark, surprised at the sincere and sober way he spoke. She began to get an inkling of the way the cowhands felt about that fence across the narrows of the Double K.

"You know how Lindon got that Land Grant?" Mark went on.

"I'm not sure," she admitted.

"On the agreement that he kept the trail open, never closed it down. That was why he got the narrows, it's good winter graze and it lets the herd run through good food without being on his main grant land too long. Now the trail's closed there can only be the one answer—war."

"Would it come to that?"

"Likely," Dusty answered. "Stone Hart's coming north, be along most any day now. He's a good man—and a damned good trail boss. He won't waste time going all that way around when he's got clear right to cross. So Wedge'll fight, and if he can't force through the men following him north'll fight. Most of that fighting'll be done over your land, not on the Double K. At the end, no matter who gets their way, no matter who wins, you small folks lose out."

"How do you mean?"

"You make a living here, not much more. You need to sell your stock to make enough to carry you through," Dusty explained. "There'll be none of that. And once the shooting starts you'll be in the middle, stock'll go, maybe folks be killed. You'll be the ones who go under and that's what I'm trying to prevent. That's why I'm waiting for the Wedge to come."

"But would your friend allow that to happen?"

"Stone makes his living running contract herds for small ranch owners like your pappy. He'll have around three thousand head along with him, six or eight spreads shipping herds. Those folks are relying on Stone, just as you are on selling your stock. He never yet let his folks down and I don't figure he aims to make a start at it now."

"Won't there be trouble when he comes anyway?" she asked, watching Dusty's face and wondering how she ever thought of him as being small.

"Maybe," replied Dusty. "Maybe not. Only I've never yet seen the hired gun who would face real opposition and we'll have that behind us with the Wedge. If we can get through, talk this out with Keller, or whatever you called him, we might show him how wrong he is."

"Never knowed a gal like you for asking questions," Mark drawled in a tone which warned her the subject must be dropped.

"And I'd bet you've known some girls," she answered.

"Couple here, couple there."

"When did you first get interested in girls, Mark?"

He grinned at her. "The day I found out they wasn't boys."

Once more the conversation took on a lighter note and continued that way until they came towards the town of Barlock, buckboard and horses making for the main street.

Barlock was neither large nor impressive. Like most towns in Texas it existed to supply the needs of the cattle industry, growing, like the State itself, out of hide and horn, beef fattened on the rolling range land. The surrounding ranches supplied year-long custom for the cowhands had no closer place in which to spend their monthly payroll. During the trail drive season added wealth could be garnered from passing herds, their crews taking a chance of a quick celebration before leaving Texas.

All this did not mean that Barlock grew larger than any other weather-washed township out on the rolling plains. There were some fifteen business premises, two stores, two saloons, the inevitable Wells Fargo office with its telegraph wires and its barns and stables, a livery barn, a small house in back of town which showed its purpose with a small, discreet, red lantern. The rest were just like any other small town might offer, being neither more nor less grand.

Mark and Dusty now rode at one side of the wagon and the girl was surprised to see how they no longer kept protectively close to it. They passed into town, going by a blacksmith's forge, then the barber's shop.

"That's the Land Office," she said, indicating the next single floor, small wooden building.

"Saloon, ma'am," Dusty replied in a louder tone than necessary. "Why thank you kindly for pointing it out."

On the porch before the Land Office lounged two tough-looking men with prominent guns and deputy marshal badges. They appeared to be loafing, yet clearly stood guard to prevent anybody entering and bothering whatever might be in the office. Neither spoke, nor did they move, but studied the passing party with cold, hard, unfriendly eyes.

"Thanks for showing us the way in ma'am," Mark went on, also speaking in a far louder tone than necessary. "Let's find us a drink, *amigo*."

"Been eating trail dust for so long I need one," Dusty replied, then in a lower voice, for they had passed the Land Agent's office. "Where at's the jail gal. Tell, don't point."

Freda's finger had started to make an instinctive point but she held it down and answered, "At the other end of town, beyond the Jackieboy Saloon."

"We're going in this place here," Dusty said. "Wait out here for us. What's in that shop opposite?"

"Dresses."

"Couldn't be better. See you soon."

They swung their horses from her side and rode to the hitching rail outside the smaller of Barlock's saloons. Freda swung her own horse towards the other side of the street and jumped down. She crossed to the window of the dress shop and stood looking in the window, admiring a dress which would cost more than she could possibly afford.

Time dragged slowly. She wondered what might be keeping Dusty and Mark for there was no sign of either man. How soon would one of Elben's deputies get suspicious and come to ask her why she waited before the saloon? For five minutes she pretended to be examining the horse's hooves and the set of its harness, then leaned by the side of the wagon looking along the street.

The tall shape of Mark Counter loomed at the batwing doors. Freda heaved a sigh of relief. Then her smile of welcome died on her face as she watched the way her two friends came into sight.

For a moment Mark and Dusty stood on the sidewalk before the saloon. Then they started to walk towards the Land Agent's office without showing a sign that either of them had ever seen her before. Their hats were thrust back and they went on unsteady legs in a manner she knew all too well. They seemed to have spent their time in the saloon gathering a fair quantity of liquid refreshment. In fact they both looked to be well on their way to rolling drunk.

Hot and angry Freda stamped her way across the street on to the sidewalk behind them. She aimed to give them a piece of her mind when she caught up with them and to hell with the consequences. They had come into town to help her and the moment they hit the main street they took off for the saloon to become a pair of drunken irresponsible cowhands. She would never have expected it of either of them, yet the evidence stood plain before her eyes.

"Yippee ti-yi-ki-yo!" Dusty whooped, sounding real drunk. "Ain't no Yankee can throw me."

"Le's find another saloon 'n' likker up good," suggested Mark Counter, making a grab at the hitching rail on the end of the Land Agent's office and holding it to get his balance, allowing Dusty to go ahead. "Another lil drink sure won't do us any harm."

From his tone and attitude he already carried enough bottled brave-maker in him to settle him down. Freda came forward, her cheeks burned hot with both shame and rage. She saw the two deputies looking towards her friends and felt the anger grow even more. Dusty and Mark were headed for trouble, she hoped they got it.

"They sure didn't waste any time," said one deputy.

"Never knowed a cowhand who did," replied the other. "Nor could handle his likker once he took it."

"That big feller looks like he might have money. Let's tell them we'll jail 'em unless they pay out a fine."

"Sure. They'll be easy enough."

Dusty Fog looked owlishly towards the two men who blocked the sidewalk ahead of him.

"Ain't no Yankee can throw me!" he stated again, belliger-
ently.

"You pair's headed for jail," answered the taller deputy.
"Come on quiet, or we'll take you with a broke head."

"Jail!" yelped Dusty, fumbling in his pants pocket. "You
can't do that to us. I got money—look."

He held out a twenty dollar gold piece before the men. Two
hands shot out greedily towards the coin, both deputies eager
to get hold of it. By an accident it seeemed Dusty let the gold
piece fall from his fingers. It rang on the sidewalk and both
deputies bent forward, reaching down to grab it.

Dusty's hands shot out fast, closed on the bending deputies'
shirt collars and heaved. They shot by on either side of him,
caught off balance and taken unprepared by the strength in
the small Texan's body.

Out of control, the two men went forward into Mark's
waiting hands which clamped on the outside of each head.
Mark brought his hands together, crashing two heads into
each other with a most satisfying thud. Both deputies went
limp as if they'd been suddenly boned. They would have fallen
to the ground only Mark gripped their collars again and held
them up, leaning them against the office wall and jamming
them there as if standing talking to them.

Turning fast, hands ready to grab at the butts of his Colts,
Dusty looked along the street. Nobody appeared to have seen
them for the street remained empty except for the girl. A girl
whose face seemed to be twisting into a variety of different
expressions. Relief, amazement, anger, amusement, they all
warred for prominence on Freda's face.

Then Dusty was grinning, not the slobbering leering grin of
a drunk, but the grin she had seen before, when he talked with
her before leaving for Barlock.

"Lordy me, gal," he said, taking her arm and leading her to
the Land Agent's door. "I'll never forget your face when we
came out of that saloon."

CHAPTER FIVE

Moral Suasion

BEFORE any of the thoughts buzzing around in Freda's head could be put to words, before she had hardly time to collect her thoughts even, she saw Dusty Fog open the door of the Land Agent's office. Freda suddenly realized the reason for the piece of play-acting. By pretending to be drunk and incapable Dusty and Mark put the watching deputies off guard and enabled the two Texans to handle the matter without fuss or disturbance.

Wondering what would come next Freda followed Dusty through the open office door, into the hallowed and protected halls of Karl Mallick, Land Agent.

The office was designed for privacy, so that the occupants could talk their business undisturbed. There was but one large room, Mallick living in Barlock's best, in fact only, hotel. All the windows had been painted black for the lower half of their length and could only have been looked through by a person standing on tiptoes and peering over the black portion. The two deputies on watch outside whenever the office was in use prevented such liberties being taken.

It was a room without fancy furnishings. Nothing more or less than a set of filing cabinets in a corner, a stout safe in another, a few chairs, a range saddle with rifle and rope in a third. In the center of the room stood a large desk and at the desk, head bent forward as he wrote rapidly on a sheet of paper, sat Karl Mallick, Land Agent and attorney for the Double K.

Mallick had much on his mind as he wrote a letter. He set down the pen and began toying with the branding iron which lay on his desk top. He heard the door open and scowled. Only

one man in town should be able to enter without knocking and
he would be hardly likely to come around in plain daylight,
not to the front door, unless something had gone bad wrong in
their plans.

Raising his head, so his black bearded face looked towards
the door, Mallick found he had visitors.

"What the—!" he began, coming to his feet as he stared at
the small man and the girl who entered.

"Just sit again, mister," Dusty answered.

Behind him Mark entered, still supporting the two deputies,
and dumped them in a heap on the floor. Mallick sat, but his
right hand shot down to pull at the drawer of his desk, getting
it open and exposing an Adams revolver which lay inside ready
for use in such emergencies.

Whatever use Mallick intended to put the gun to never came
off. Dusty let Freda's arm free and he lunged forward fast.
His right hand trapped Mallick's left wrist as it lay on the desk
top. With his left hand, gripping it between his second and
third fingers, Dusty caught up the pen Mallick had laid aside.
Moving faster than Mallick had ever seen, Dusty inserted
the pen between the bearded man's two middle fingers. Then
Dusty closed his hand, gripping down hard. With his hand
scant inches from the butt of the Adams revolver Mallick
stopped as if he'd run against an invisible wall. Pain, numb-
ing, savage, agonizing pain rammed through his trapped
hand. He could not cry out. All he could do was claw the right
hand from the desk drawer and reach towards Dusty's trap-
ping fingers.

Dusty released the hold before Mallick's hand reached his.
He stepped around the desk, took out the Adams and thrust it
into his waist band. Then he moved back and took his first
look at the Land Agent.

Although he was tall and bulky Mallick did not give the impression of being a really hard man. He wore a good eastern
style suit, white shirt and a neck-tie of sober hue. His face,
what showed of it from behind the black beard, looked like
the face of a man who spent some of his time out under the
sun, which might be expected in his job. The eyes were light
blue, cold and at the moment filled with hate as he studied his
visitors.

He did not have the look of a western man.

Slowly his hand dropped towards the branding iron.

Having closed the door Mark Counter stepped forward and took up the heavy iron, handling it like a child's toy. He looked down at Mallick as he stepped back holding the iron between his hands, left below the handle, right at the head.

"Lead us not into temptation," Mark drawled, "just like the good book says. Feller tried to hit me with one of these things, one time when he got riled."

"What do you pair want here?" Mallick snarled, his accent sounding eastern. New York most likely from the way he spoke. "This's private property. You could be jailed for attacking those deputies and coming in here."

"Why *hombre*," replied Mark calmly. "We found these two gents all a-swooning away in the heat and hauled them in."

"And it's a trio, not us pair," Dusty went on. "You likely know Miss Lasalle. Her pappy came in to see you this morning. Allows anybody wants to trade at the store has to come and get a note from you."

"Where'd you hear a fool tale like that?" growled Mallick.

"I just told you *hombre*," Dusty answered, his nostrils quivering as he sniffed the air suspiciously. He threw a glance first at Mark, then at Freda. "Whooee! I thought that bay rum you used was strong, Mark."

"That's not mine," replied Mark, also sniffing.

"Don't look at me either," Freda gasped, also sniffing the sickly sweet aroma which aroused Dusty's interest. She was both surprised and puzzled by it and laid the blame on some lady visitor to Mallick, only if she used that kind of perfume she was not likely to be a lady.

"Smells like a Dodge City blacksmith's," drawled Mark.

"You ought to know," Freda answered, then blushed. A young lady should be unaware of the fact that a blacksmith, used in the way Mark spoke, had nothing to do with shoeing horses, but rather as acting as a pimp for ladies of easy virtue.

"I've better things to do than listen to you lot jawing," snarled Mallick, wanting the subject changed, although not for the obvious reason.

"That's where you're wrong, mister," Dusty drawled quietly. "You never had anything so important as seeing that we get the note to the store. See, old Mark here's an easy-going boy when he's fed. Trouble being we're staying out at Freda's place and they're short on food. And when Mark gets hungry he gets mean and riled.''

"Which same I'm getting hunger on me right now."

Saying this Mark raised the branding iron before him and tightened his grip. At first none of the others could see any sign, except in the way Mark's face became set and grim. Then slowly, before the surprised eyes of Mallick and Freda, the stout iron bar began to bend. Freda saw the strain on Mark's face, saw the way his shirt sleeves, roomy as they were, went taut against the swell of his biceps as they rose and writhed under the pressure he put on. The bar began to bend, take the shape of a C, then an O. Not until it bent around in a full circle did Mark stop his pressure and toss the branding iron down before Mallick.

"Yes, sir," he said. "I can feel the hunger coming on right now."

Mallick made no reply. He stared down at the branding iron and the pallor which came to his face showed he appreciated the situation in full. Through all the Panhandle country he doubted if more than one man could equal the display of strength he just witnessed.

Footsteps sounded outside the building, and over the blackened lower part of the window showed a familiar hat's top. Mallick recognized it and so did Freda but she kept quiet. She did not need to speak, the flicker of relief which passed across Mallick's face warned Dusty and Mark, told them all they needed to know. The footsteps came to a halt before the door and a knock sounded.

"Mr. Mallick!" called a voice. "You all right, the boys aren't out here."

Even as Mallick started to rise, opening his mouth to utter a yell to the man outside, his plan failed. Dusty's left hand flipped across his body, the white handled Army Colt left his holster, its seven and a half inch barrel thrusting up to poke a yawning muzzle under Mallick's chin, at the same instant the hammer clicked back under Dusty's thumb.

"Get rid of him!" Dusty warned in a savage whisper, "or you'll be talking without a top to your head."

Mallick hired paid killers, men who sold their gun-skill to the highest bidders. He knew such men would never hesitate to carry out such a threat as Dusty made. Nor, looking at the small Texan's grim face, did he doubt but that his slightest hesitation would see a bullet crashing in his head. Mallick slumped back into his chair, sweat pouring down his face as he opened his mouth. He tried to keep his voice normal, and yet still convey a warning that things were wrong to the man outside. He hoped that for once in his life Elben the town marshal might show some sign of sense.

"It's all right, marshal," he called. "I told them to go along to the saloon."

Much to Mallick's relief the words prevented Elben from entering the room. He hoped the marshal might be following his usual practice of spending the afternoon in the saloon and would miss the two men, then mention the fact to the boss who would form his own conclusions and have a party down this way fast.

In this Mallick was to be disappointed. Elben shrugged, knowing no important business to be taking place inside. He strolled on, passing around the end of the building and heading down to the small house with the red light, having some civic duty to attend to, the collection of his weekly contribution from the madame to what they referred as election campaign expenses. From the house he returned, after a time to the jail.

While Elben attended to his self-appointed duties Mallick, one of the men who employed him, sat in the Land Agent's office hoping against hope that help would come.

"Write!" Dusty snapped, pointing to the pen and paper. "Make it *pronto*!"

Mallick did not argue. He had worked himself up the path to defiance when he saw Elben's hat passing the window. Only Dusty had pricked the balloon before it could be used and Mallick had nothing left with which to be defiant. He threw a glance to where Mark Counter took the rope from his own saddle, went towards the moaning deputies and began making a good fastening job on them. Then he took up the pen and began to write.

Having watched everything with puzzled, then smiling interest, Freda turned to Dusty and asked:

"Is that what you call moral suasion?"

"Rio Hondo style," Dusty agreed, taking the paper Mallick

wrote out and the letter, comparing the signatures on them. "It'll do. Hawg-tie him, Mark."

"Like a hawg," Mark agreed, gagging the deputies with their own bandanas. "I picked up your double eagle, out there, Dusty, want it back?"

"My need's greater than your'n," Dusty answered. "But keep it to send a telegraph message to Uncle Devil for me after we leave here."

With hands long skilled in securely tying things, Mark flipped the rope around Mallick's shoulders. Dusty sat on the edge of the desk and watched the hog-tying process, he also started to question Mallick.

"Like to see your boss," he began.

"He's not here yet," Mallick replied.

"When'd he be coming out here?"

"I don't know."

"Who ordered the fence built?" Dusty asked.

"Keller did!"

"You said he wasn't here," Freda pointed out.

"He sent a telegraph message. Told me to buy you folks out and fence his property."

"How long have you been out west, *hombre*?" Mark asked, quickly securing the man's wrists together.

"Long enough."

"You know how us folks feel about wire?" Dusty went on.

"Yeah. But Keller ordered me to lay it."

"He doesn't know how much land he's got then?" Mark said, thinking how much wiring a vast spread like the Double K would cost.

Mallick surged against the ropes and the expression which flickered across his face at the words surprised Dusty. Although he did not know what might have caused it the words had hit Mallick hard. Dusty could read facial expressions and knew fear when he saw it. He saw it this time in the bearded face of the Land Agent. Mallick threw a look at the wastepaper basket, then jerked his eyes away once more. Yet he left it too late. Dusty followed the direction of the other man's gaze. The basket contained only a small pile of pieces of paper as if a man idly ripped up something and tossed it in. Only an idle action and odd scraps of paper would not bring the fear and desperation to Mallick's face.

Bending down Dusty scooped the paper from the basket.
Mallick gave a snarl of rage and struggled impotently against
the securing ropes, but Mark held him down and Freda
jumped forward with her own handkerchief to gag him. Once
more the girl proved herself capable of cool and fast thought
for neither Dusty nor Mark gave her any sign of needing help.

"What is it?" she asked.

Dusty spread open the crumpled torn pile of paper and
looked down at it.

"A map of some kind. It'll take time to fit all this together
right and we don't have time to spare, gal. I'll take it with
me."

Fear, hate and worse showed in Mallick's eyes as he struggled impotently against the taut ropes which held him fast. He
felt himself lifted to his feet, hauled into a corner where he
could not be seen from the windows, then sat with his back
against the wall while Mark lashed his ankles together. Mark
knew his business, knew the discovery of Mallick and his
crowd might mean death for the girl, Dusty and himself. So
Mark aimed to see discovery was less likely. He dragged the
now conscious and groaning deputies to where Mallick sat,
propped them against the wall and used the last of the Agent's
rope to secure their feet together. They now sat tied in line and
it would be unlikely, if not impossible, that they could manage
to roll, wriggle or crawl out into view, or even to where by
kicking or stamping against the walls they might attract attention.

Freda crossed the room and looked down at the three bound
men.

"We won't be selling, Mr. Mallick," she said.

"Let's go, gal," Dusty drawled, watching Mark lock and
bolt the rear door.

Cautiously Freda started to open the front door, meaning to
peer out and make sure their departure would be undetected.
This action did not meet with Dusty's approval.

"Go on straight out, gal," he ordered. "Act like you've
been to see Mallick on business, not like you're robbing the
bank."

Holding down the comment which bubbled at her lips Freda
stepped through the door. She had no sooner got outside than
a hand caught her arm and turned her. She gave a muffled

squeak, felt herself scooped up into Mark's arms. His face came down, lips crushing her own in a kiss. The girl struggled, her little hands hitting Mark on the shoulders. Then he released her and she staggered back a pace. Her right hand came around in a slap which jerked his head aside.

"Just because I talk friendly—" she began hotly.

"When you pair of love-birds have done," Dusty put in. "I've locked the door and we can move off."

Freda's angry outburst faded, contrition came to her face. Then she flushed red and glared at the two men. Mark put a hand to his cheek and grinned.

"That's a mean right hand you've got, gal."

"I'm sorry," she replied. "But you might have warned me. I've heard about you."

"Yeah," grinned Mark. "I could feel it. Anyway it spoils things when the gal knows what she's going to get. I'll see to getting word to Ole Devil and you take care of Russian Olga here, Dusty."

"Who's Russian Olga?" Freda asked, watching Mark walk along the sidewalk making for the Wells Fargo office, while Dusty headed her across the street towards the waiting buckboard.

"She's a gal we saw one time,"* Dusty replied. "Claims to be the female fist fighting champion of the world, only she got licked that time."

"Girls fist f— You're jobbing me!"

"Nope. There's a few of them about. Get the buckboard and head for the store and when we get inside don't be surprised at how I act. I don't want anybody thinking we're friends."

"Scared I might ruin you socially?" she asked with a smile.

"Call it that," grinned Dusty in reply. "That slap you gave Mark'd've helped if anybody was watching, wouldn't make you look real friendly with us. Only we had to stop anybody seeing me lock the door and Mark reckoned kissing you'd be as good a way of hiding me as any."

"And I slapped his face, poor Mark."

"He'll live."

Freda remembered where Mark was headed and a thought struck her.

* Told of in QUIET TOWN

"Won't your Uncle Devil object to your neglecting your work?"

"He'll turn the air blue and blister my hide, but he'll be behind me all the way and if this thing blows too big he'll get help here, happen we send for it. Now get in the buggy—and remember, gal, you've just been made to sell your home. Act like it, don't look so all-fired pleased with yourself."

When Freda entered Roylan's store she looked dejected almost on the verge of tears. Matt Roylan, sleeved rolled up to expose his muscular arms, leaned his big bulky, powerful frame on the counter and looked across the room towards the door. The lean, gun-hung hard-case with the deputy's badge also looked. He leaned by the cracker barrel into which he dipped his hand at regular intervals. His eyes studied the girl, then went to Dusty who followed on her heels.

"Supply her," Dusty ordered as they reached the counter.

"Says which?" asked the gunman.

"You want to see the paper?"

Dusty made his reply with a cold smile flickering on his lips. The lanky gunman studied Dusty, reading the signs in the matched guns, in those well-made holsters and the workmanship of the gunbelt. He knew quality when he saw it—and he saw it in the small Texan. Without knowing who Dusty was, the gunman knew what he was. Dusty belonged to the real fast guns, one of the magic handed group who could draw and shoot in less than half a second.

For his part Dusty tried to give the impression of being a typical hired hard-case, a man who used a brace of real fast guns to off-set his lack of inches. From the looks on the gunman and Roylan's faces Dusty had made his point, they took him at face value.

"You one of the boys from the spread?" asked the gunman, meaning to be sociable. "Mallick hire you?"

"Go ask him," Dusty answered in an uncompromising tone.

Watching from the corner of her eye Freda felt amazed at the change in Dusty. He seemed to be able to turn himself from an insignificant cowhand to any part he wanted to play. Right now, happen she didn't know him, she would have taken him for a brash, cocky and tough hired gunhand who knew he had the other man over a barrel in more ways than one. She saw that neither Roylan nor the deputy doubted that Dusty brought her from Mallick's office after forcing her father to sell out.

"You and your father are leaving after all, Freda," Roylan said, a touch of sadness in his voice as he looked at the note Dusty tossed in a contemptuous manner before him. His voice held such genuine sadness that Freda felt guilty at having to deceive him, yet she knew she did not dare take a chance on letting hint of her true position slip out.

"She's leaving, *hombre,*" answered Dusty, saving Freda from needing to lie. "So shake the bull-droppings from your socks and make with some service."

In his own right Matt Roylan could be a tough, hard man. However he knew the futility of tangling with Double K in what now amounted to their town. He might jump the two hired hard-cases, lick them, although the small one looked fast enough to throw lead into him before he could bat an eye. Even if he did manage to lick the two men and throw them out, the Double K held his bank-note and would foreclose on him.

So Roylan stared to collect the order Freda gave him. Yet somehow, as he worked, Roylan got the feeling that Freda was not quite so grief-stricken as she tried to appear. The girl could not act well enough to continue her pose, at least not well enough to fool an old friend like Roylan. The storekeeper noticed this and felt puzzled by it. He threw a glance at Dusty who sat by the counter and dipped a hand into the candy jar to take one out. Roylan couldn't think how, but somehow Freda had gathered the note from Mallick, the girl was all right and things not so black as they looked. That would be impossible—unless the small Texan was not what he seemed. Yet he had the mannerisms of a tough hard-case hired gun.

One thing Roylan knew for sure, with the note from Mallick and the presence of one of the Double K's toughs, he stood in the clear. If it came out later that Freda managed to trick the paper from Mallick in some way all the blame could be laid on the deputy who accepted the note as genuine.

"How long've you been with Double K?" asked the gun-hand, giving Dusty a long and curious stare.

"Not long," Dusty answered truthfully. "You always this nosey?"

The gunman grunted and relapsed into silence once more, except for the crunching of the cracker he took out of the barrel. He did not know all the men out at the Double K but knew Mallick hired efficient men when he could find them, and this small Texan looked and acted efficient. One thing the deputy knew for sure. The Texan wouldn't take to having his word doubted and could likely deal harshly with any man who doubted it.

Freda felt tension rising inside her with every minute. She watched Roylan collecting the goods from the shelves. He seemed to be taking his time and she wanted to beg him to hurry. At any moment Mallick would be found and the alarm given. Then Dusty and Mark would need to face a hostile town, or at least such a part of the town as felt under obligation to Double K.

At last the order had been gathered and she paid for it. Then Roylan began to box it and carry it to her buckboard. Dusty watched this. The load did not look much after seeing the OD Connected's cook collect a chuckwagon full at a time, but the Lasalle family did not need such quantities of food and what they now had would be the difference between survival and being driven out.

Freda left the store, wanting to be outside so that she might see what happened around town. The gathering of supplies had taken some time and she thought Mark might be making his way towards her, but at first she saw no sign. Then Mark and another man left the Jackieboy Saloon. She saw Elben the town marshal and others she recognized as his deputies surround the pair in a menacing half-circle. A pair of riders came slowly along the street into town, beyond the Jackieboy Saloon but Freda gave them no second glance. She stared at the men before the saloon for another moment. Then she turned and darted back into the store.

"Dusty!" she gasped. "Mark's in trouble."

CHAPTER SIX

The Ysabel Kid Meets A Lady

HOLDING his big white stallion to a mile devouring trot the Ysabel Kid rode north. He found and now followed the signs of last year's drives with no difficulty for the sign lay plain for a man to see.

Ahead lay the fence. The Kid saw it and a frown came to his brow. Like Dusty and Mark he hated fences of any kind, probably more so than his friends for they would grudgingly admit some fences had their uses. To the Kid any kind of fence was an anathema. The free-ranging blood of his forefathers, all breeds which never took to being fettered and walled in, revolted against the sight of anything which might bring an end to the open range.

Touching the white's flanks the Kid swung to one side, heading down the stream which marked the boundary of Double K and which carried the barbed wire on the bank he rode along. Likely Double K had men watching the fence and he did not want to be delayed in obeying Dusty's orders while he made war.

The wire ended at a point where the stream made a sharp curve and formed the end of the narrows. After scanning the area the Kid allowed Blackie to wade into and through the water. At the other side he set his course across the narrows, in the correct direction, with the ease of a sailor using a compass to navigate his ship. All the range ahead of him looked good, plenty of grass, enough water, and dotted with small woods in which the cattle might shelter during bad weather. A man who owned such a spread should have no need to jump his neighbors' land for more grazing.

Caution had always been a by-word for the Kid. A man

didn't live as he'd lived during his formative years* without developing the instincts and caution of a lobo wolf. Not even in times of peace and on the safe ranges of the OD Connected did the Ysabel Kid ride blindly and blithely along. Always there was caution, always his eyes and ears stayed alert for any slight warning sound or flickering sight which might herald the coming of danger.

So the two men who appeared on a rim half a mile off to his right did not take the Kid by surprise. He heard one of them yell, saw them set spurs to work and send their horses forward at a gallop. As yet he did not speed up the big white stallion. Blackie could allow the men to come in much closer before he need increase his pace any. The Kid knew his horse could easily leave behind the mounts of the Double K men, happen he felt like it. One word would see the white running away from the pursuers, leaving them behind as if they had lead weights lashed to their legs.

"Couldn't catch up even if they wanted to, old Blackie hoss," drawled the Kid. "Which same they want to, and are trying to."

After dispensing this rather left-handed cowboy logic the Kid relaxed in his saddle. When the two men passed behind a clump of bushes out of sight for a few moments he bent and drew his rifle from the saddleboot. With the old "yellowboy" in his hands he knew he could handle the two men and prevent their coming close enough to bother him.

There had been a time, just after the War, when the Kid's handling of the pursuit would have been far different. Then he would have found cover and used his old Mississippi rifle (he did not own a Winchester Model of 1866 "yellowboy" rifle in those days) to down one of the following pair for sure and probably both if the other did not take the hint. Those days ended on the Brownsville trail when he met the man who turned him from a border smuggler into a useful member of society. It had been Dusty Fog who prevented the Kid sliding into worse forms of law-breaking than the running of contraband and gave him a slightly higher idea of the value of human life. So the Kid contented himself in having the rifle ready. If the men became too intrusive he could easily take steps to dis-

---

* Told of in COMANCHE

courage them, but he aimed to let them make the first move.

For a mile the Kid rode at the same pace and the men, knowing the futility of trying to close with him and his fast moving horse, clung to his trail like a pair of buzzards watching a trail herd for weak steers dropping out. Only the Kid was no weak steer, he didn't aim to get caught or to drop out.

A woman's scream shattered the air, coming from a small *bosque,* a clump of trees to the Kid's right. He brought the big white stallion to a halt, looking in the direction of the sound. It might be a trick to lure him close, to hold him for the two following men, only that scream sounded a whole lot too good for pretence. Then his ears caught another sound, low, menacing, one which set Blackie fiddle-footing nervously. The hunting snarl of an angry cougar.

Without a thought of the following gunmen, the Kid headed his big white horse forward fast, making for the *bosque*. Once more the scream rang out, than he saw, among the trees, what caused the terror.

The young woman stood back up against a tree, her face pale, her mouth open for another scream. On top of a rock, facing her, crouched for a spring, with its tail lashing back and forwards, was a big, old, tom cougar. To one side, reins tangled in a blue-berry bush, fighting wildly to get free, eyes rolling in terror, a fine looking bay horse raised enough noise to effectively cover the sound of the approaching white stallion and its rider.

Only rarely would a cougar, even one as big as the old tom, chance attacking a human being without the incentive of real hunger and the human being bad hurt, or without being cornered. Probably the cougar had its eye on horse-flesh, it's favorite food, and would have ignored the young woman. However fear carries its own distinctive scent and the cougar caught it, knowing the human being feared it. So the big tom changed its mind, decided to take the woman as being an even easier kill than the horse.

Bringing his brass-framed Winchester to his shoulder the Kid sighted and fired all in one incredibly swift move. The cougar had caught some sound Blackie made and swung its head to investigate the new menace. Even before its cat-quick reactions could carry it in a long bound to safety at one side, the cougar took lead. The Winchester spat out, throwing back

echoes from the surrounding trees, the cougar gave out with a
startled squalling wail, sprang from the rock, back arched in
pain and hurling at the young woman.

Moving so fast the lever looked almost like a blur the Ysabel
Kid threw two more shots into the cougar, spinning it around
in the air and dropping it in a lifeless heap almost at her feet.
The young woman stared down, trying to back further into the
tree trunk, not knowing she need no longer fear the animal.

"You all right, ma'am?" asked the Kid, coming down from
Blackie, landing before the girl and holding his rifle ready.

For a long moment she did not reply. She stood with her
face against the trees, not sobbing or making any sound, just
frozen rigid with the reaction of her narrow escape. Then with
an almost physical effort, she seemed to get control of herself
and turned towards him.

"Yes, thank you," she said in an accent which sounded
alien and strange to the Kid's ears. "I'm afraid I was rather
foolish. Mr. Dune told me there were mountain lions in this
area, but I'd always heard they don't attack human beings."

"Don't often," replied the Kid, knowing she wanted to
talk, to shake the last of her fear away. "This'n most likely
was hungry and figured you'd make an easier meal than the
hoss."

Holding the "yellowboy" in his right hand and sweeping
off the black Stetson with his left, the Kid looked at the girl his
timely arrival saved. Without a doubt she was one of the most
beautiful young women he had ever seen. Maybe a mite taller
than a man'd want, but not so tall as to appear gawky and
awkward. She had hair as black as his own, neat and tidily
cared for. Her face would draw admiring glances in any company and she'd come second to none in the beauty stakes. Her
eyes, now the fear left them, looked warm, yet not bold. She
wore a black eastern riding habit of a kind he had never seen
before. A top hat sat on her head and a veil trailed down from
the brim to fasten on to her jacket belt. Her outfit did nothing
to hide the fact that she was a very shapely young woman.

She dusted herself off, knocking the leaves from her dress.
"He took me by surprise, my horse took fright and tossed me
off. You came just in time. Thank you."

"It wasn't nothing," replied the Kid, feeling just a shade
uncomfortable in her presence.

"I can't remember ever having seen you around the ranch," she went on. "Of course Papa and I only arrived two days ago and I haven't met all the sta—cowhands yet. Mr. Dune warned me about the cougar, but I wanted to see one close up."

"Likely this old tom," replied the Kid with a grin, stirring the dead cougar with his toe, "wanted to see a real live gal close up, too."

For an instant a slight frown came to the young woman's face, then it was replaced by a smile. When the Ysabel Kid grinned in that manner he looked about fourteen years old and as innocent as a pew-full of choirboys who had put tintacks on the organ player's chair. No woman, especially one as young as this, could resist such a smile. She smiled also, it made her look even more beautiful.

The Kid looked to the young woman. From the way she talked she must be the Double K's new boss's daughter. He decided to ask if this was correct, then try and explain the dangers of putting fences around property, especially across what had always been an open trail.

Only he did not get a chance. The big white stallion swung its head in the direction they'd come, letting out a warning snort. It stood with ears pricked and nostrils working, looking for all the world like a wild animal. Reading the warning, the Kid turned fast, but he did not try to raise his rifle for he stood under the guns of the two men who followed him across the range.

"Just stay right where you are, cownurse!" one ordered.

The Kid stood fast, only he didn't let his rifle fall. He kept it in his hand, muzzle pointing to the ground, but ready for use. Then the girl stepped forward, coming between the Kid and the two men. She brought a worried look to two faces for the men could not shoot without endangering her life.

"It's all right," she said. "The young man saved my life, prevented a mountain lion from attacking me."

Still the two men did not lower their weapons, nor relax. The taller made a gesture towards the Kid.

"He's not one of our riders, Miss Keller," he said.

"Aren't you?" she asked, turned towards the Kid. "I suppose you're trespassing really, but we can overlook it this time. Put away your guns, please."

For all her strange sounding accent she made it clear that when she gave an order she expected it to be obeyed. The Kid watched the men and the girl, thinking how her tone sounded like Dusty's cousin, Betty Hardin, the voice of a self-willed young woman who was full used to be obeyed. Her last words had been directed to the two men.

They scowled, clearly not liking the idea, but holstering their guns for all of that. Their duty was to patrol the range and discourage stray drifters from crossing. Neither had seen Tring's discomforted bunch returning from the abortive raid on Lasalle's place and did not know anything about the Kid's part in it. They did know that they should have stopped him getting this far in. They should also most definitely have never allowed him to get so close to Norma Keller, only daughter of the new owner of the Double K. However Norma had given orders and they were instructed to obey her.

Norma turned to the Kid and looked him over with some interest. Once more he felt like a bashful schoolboy—then he remembered, in the early days he felt just the same when Betty Hardin looked at him.

"What are you doing on my father's land?" she asked coolly.

"Just passing through, ma'am, headed north to Bent's Ford, that's over the Indian Nation line a piece."

"I know!" she answered. "Do you make a habit of riding across other people's property?"

For a moment anger flickered in the Kid's eyes. Then he remembered that the girl was English, likely they did things a mite different over there. Only now she was in Texas and would need to change some of her ideas. He held down his angry reply and said:

"This here's always been open range country, ma'am. In Texas folks don't stop a stranger from crossing their land as long as he does no damage and makes no grief for the owners."

"I see," replied the girl, and her entire tone had changed. "Of course one must remember this is a new—I'm sorry if I snapped. Never let it be said the Keller family failed to conform with the local custom. Would you care to come to the ranch and allow father to thank you in a more suitable manner?"

For an instant the two men looked relieved, but the Kid shook his head.

"Thank you, no, ma'am," he replied. "I've got to make Bent's Ford as soon as I can. Got me a riding chore out from there and I can't miss it. Say, whyn't you have these boys here skin out that ole cougar, or tote it back to your place and have it done. It'll make a dandy footrug and you'll likely have a story to tell folks about it."

"Why yes, that's a good idea," she answered and turned to the men. "Will you attend to it, please?"

The word "please" might be there, but the Kid got the idea the girl aimed to have her orders carried out for all of being polite. He knew he could now ride on without needing to bother about the two men. He held his rifle in both hands, ready to handle any refusal, or try at holding him, but the men turned to walk towards the cougar.

Quickly the Kid swung afork his big stallion. He booted the rifle, removed his hat once more and gave Norma an elegant salute.

"*Adios*, ma'am," he said, watching the two men.

"Good-bye," she answered, looking at the white with appreciation showing in her eyes for she knew a good horse when she saw one. "If you are ever in this part of the country again drop in and see us. My father would be pleased to meet you."

"I'll do just that, ma'am," the Kid replied, setting his hat on his head.

Turning his horse the Kid rode out of the *bosque* and headed north once more, making for Bent's Ford. He knew neither of the men would follow him now, they would be too busy with the cougar. However the Double K might have more riders on it, men who also aimed to keep strangers away. He allowed Blackie to make a better pace and did not relax, not even after he left the narrows and passed over the Texas line into the Indian Nations.

Norma Keller watched the two men as they profanely tried to load the cougar on to one of their horses, a horse which showed a marked reluctance at having anything at all to do with such a creature. Then she went to her own horse and calmed it down feeling annoyed that she had not cared for the animal earlier. Not until she managed to quieten the horse and freed it did her eyes go back to the men. By now they had managed to get the cougar's body across the back of the horse and lashed it into place.

A smile flickered across her face as she thought of the innocent looking boy whose arrival saved her life. He looked quite friendly and so young to handle a rifle so well. The three holes in the cougar's body (she smiled as she found herself no longer using the term mountain lion) could be covered by the palm of her hand and any one would have proved fatal. She hoped the holes could be covered and somebody could tan and cure the skin for her.

The smile stayed as she thought of the way that the youngster spoke. She made a mental note to remember this was not the East Riding of Yorkshire, but a new country with different ways. In England no worker would have dared address her on such terms of equality and she found the sensation stimulating. Norma Keller was no snob. The upper-class to which she belonged rarely were snobs, that was the privilege of the newly-rich, the intellectuals who felt unsure of their position in life. She felt no snobbish class-distinction against the Kid, nor any annoyance at the way in which he addressed her. He spoke politely, yet without in any way being subservient. She wondered who he was, where he came from, what his position in life might be. Then she smiled still more. It would be highly unlikely that she ever met the boy again. Or was he such a boy? He seemed to be ageless. She wished she might get to know him better. He seemed to be so much better natured and pleasant than the rather sullen men hired by Mr. Mallick while she and her father travelled from their home in England, the home they would never return to again.

"All set, Miss Keller," growled one of the men.

"Good," she replied, allowing him to help her mount to the side-saddle she used. "Let's get that creature home before it stiffens and can't be skinned."

They rode back through the *bosque* and out at the far side. Norma threw her eyes over the range, searching for some sign of her rescuer, but seeing none. So she rode with the two men, comparing them with him and not to their advantage. There was so much she wanted to know about this new land, so much they might have taught her, but they seemed sullen and uncommunicative.

For a mile or so they rode in silence, then she saw a rider top
a rim and head towards them, a man who looked familiar.

"That's Mr. Dune, isn't it?" she asked.

"Yeah," grunted the taller man. "That Dune all right."

Norma frowned for she did not approve of employees refer-
ring in such a manner to their foreman. However she made no
comment for Norma had already seen a different standard of
behaviour seemed common in this new land she and her father
picked for their home.

Coming up at a gallop Dune brought his horse to a sliding
halt, eager to impress Norma with his riding skill. He was
something of a range-country dandy and fashion-plate,
dressed to the height of cowhand fashion. Although only a
medium-sized man Buck Dune fancied himself as quite a lady-
killer, a gallant with a string of conquests which covered the
length and breadth of the west.

Since the girl's arrival at the ranch Dune had tried to bear
down on her with the full force of his charm and personality.
Her father had money, more money than Dune could ever recollect seeing at one time and Dune was more than willing to
find acceptance into the Keller family circle. Only the charm
which attracted girls in the better class saloons, dancehalls and
cat-houses; plus a few women not from that class but who
should have shown better sense; failed where Norma Keller
was concerned. Towards him the girl displayed a cool attitude.
She always answered his greetings, asked questions and
listened with interest to his answers but always with calm
detachment, oblivious to his swarthy good looks, his neatly
trimmed moustache, or the faint scent of bay rum which
always clung to him. She treated him as a valued employee and
made it plain that was how things would remain.

This morning the girl's flat refusal to allow him to act as her
guide when she went riding left him feeling as awkward and
shambling as a barefooted yokel boy. It had been an unusual
feeling and he still did not know if he liked it or not.

"Howdy, Miss Keller," he greeted, removing his hat in a
graceful gesture guaranteed to prove his genteel upbringing.
Then his eyes went to the cougar's body. "Where did you get
that cat?"

"I had an adventure," she replied, smiling and forgetting

that he warned her of the presence of cougars on the range. She did not notice his surprise at seeing the one her rescuer had killed. "A young man shot it when it tried to attack me."

Dune threw a glance at the two gunmen. He had clean forgotten warning the girl about the danger of mountain lions. It had been no more than an excuse to get Norma to accept his offer of guidance and company. Now it seemed she had really met up with a cougar and he lost the chance of acting as a gallant heroic rescuer.

He forgot that matter in something more urgent. His eyes stayed on the two gunmen but he remembered just in time not to say too much before the girl. If the young man was no more than a drifting cowhand it would not be too bad, for he would be unlikely to return.

"You'd best get it right back to the spread and skin it out," he said, hoping the men would read his words right.

It seemed they did, for the one toting the cougar started his horse forward, Norma at his side. The other man held his mount back, reading the message in Dune's eyes.

"Who was he?" growled Dune after the girl had ridden away.

"Some kid on a damned great white hoss," replied the other man. "It sure could move. We saw it from half a mile back and hadn't gone two hundred yards afore we knew there wasn't a chance in hell of us catching up to him."

An explosive snorted curse left Dune's lips. He let the veneer of charm fall from him and showed what he really was, a killer without moral or scruple. Tring's bunch had returned to the spread, most of them toting shotgun lead and cursing about it, although all might have accounted themselves lucky the gun carried no worse than birdshot which did no more than pierce their hides.

They gave livid and profane descriptions of the trio of men who, according to them, jumped them, held them under guns and pinned down helpless. Dune found the descriptions tallied with three men he had heard much of, although had never met up with. He remembered the Ysabel Kid, the descriptions he'd heard of that tall, dangerous young man. The descriptions often contained references to the Kid's horse, a seventeen-hand white stallion which could run like the wind.

"A tall, young looking, dark faced kid, dressed all in black?" he asked savagely. "Got him a Dragoon Colt and a bowie knife."

"That's him."

"And that's the Ysabel Kid!" snarled Dune, spitting the words out like they burned his mouth. "Which way'd he go?"

"Said he was headed for Bent's Ford."

"Reckon he was?"

"That's what he said. Was headed north all right when we put him up."

The two men sat their horses for a moment. Dune dropped a hand to the butt of the Tranter revolver holstered at his side. If the Ysabel Kid was headed for Bent's Ford he was going for some good purpose. Dusty Fog wouldn't send off his left bower* at such a time without good cause. And the Kid had seen Norma Keller. He had seen far too much to be left alive.

"I'll take your hoss, ride a relay after him!" growled Dune.

"And leave me afoot?" answered the other.

"Shout to your pard. Tell him I've got to go into Barlock in a hurry, that's for Miss Keller to hear. They can send another hoss out from the spread."

"What'll I tell Mallick, happen he comes out and wants to see you?" asked the gunman, swinging from his saddle.

"Tell him I've gone to Bent's Ford. That black dressed breed's seen a damned sight too much. He's got to be killed!"

* Left bower. Originally a term used in playing Euchre and meaning the second highest trump.

CHAPTER SEVEN

Jackieboy Disraeli

IN all fairness to Mark Counter it must be said he did not intend to get into any trouble at all.

After visiting the Wells Fargo office and sending a telegraph message which would eventually be delivered to the OD Connected house in the Rio Hondo country, Mark headed towards where he could see Freda's buckboard halted before the general store. In so doing he had to pass the hospitable doors of the Jackieboy Saloon. He saw that Dusty had collected both their horses and taken them down to the store and so would not have wasted time entering the saloon if it had not been for what he saw happening inside.

Mark glanced through the batwing doors, then came to a halt. He was a cowhand, a good one, he was also a cowhand who had seen the treatment handed out to less fortunate members of his trade when they found themselves in a saloon and at odds with the owners.

None of the crowd looked at Mark as he entered. Their full attention centered on the group at the bar. It was this same group at the bar which brought Mark into the room in the first place.

There were three men in the center of the bar, only they hadn't come to it for pleasure, or if the cowhand of the group had he sure didn't look like he was getting any of it.

"The boss told you to clear out of this section. There ain't no work here!"

The speaker stood tall, as tall as Mark Counter and maybe thirty or forty pounds heavier. From the slurred manner of his speech and the battered aspect of his face he had done more than his fair share of fist-fighting in the raw, brutal bare-knuckle manner. He had powerful arms and big hands, and was putting both to good use as he held the cowhand pressed back against the bar.

Held with the huge man's powerful hands gripping, gouging into his shoulders, the cowhand could do little. He stood six foot, had good shoulders and lean waist but he looked like a midget in the hands of the burly brutal bruiser who held him. His face twisted in agony. It was cheerful most times, maybe not too handsome, but friendly and pleasant. His clothes looked northern range fashion, they were not over-expensive, but his hat and boots both cost good money and his gunbelt, while not being a fast-man's rig, did not look like a decoration.

Standing to one side of the others a small, tubby man watched everything with drooling lips and a sadistic gaze. He was a sallow skinned man, his nose slightly large and bent. He wore a light dove-grey cutaway jacket of gambler's style, snow white trousers down which ran a black stripe, primrose yellow spats and a pair of shoes which shone enough to reflect the view around him. His shirt bore considerable frills and lace to it and his bow-tie had an almost feminine look about it. He stood relaxed at the bar, his posture nearer that a dancehall girl than of a gambling man. Taking a lace handkerchief from his cuff he mopped his brow.

"He understands now, Knuckles," he lisped in a falsetto voice which might have brought down derision on him, but did not. "Let him free."

On the order Knuckles released his hold. The young cowhand showed he had sand to burn. His right fist lashed around, smashing into the side of the huge man's bristle-covered jaw. It was a good blow, swung with weight behind it, but Knuckles did not even give a sign of knowing it landed. He grunted and his big left hand came back, slashing into the cowhand's cheek and sprawling him to the floor.

"He's not learned his lesson, Knuckles!" purred the tubby man. "Stomp him!"

Like an elephant moving Knuckles stepped towards the dazed cowhand, lifting a huge foot ready to obey. Through the pain mists the cowhand saw Knuckles towering over him, tried to force himself into some kind of action.

Two hands descended on Knuckles's shoulders. He felt him-

self heaved back and propelled violently away from the bar. A
mutter of surprise ran through the saloon as the huge bouncer
went reeling and staggering backwards. Not one of the watching crowd had expected to see a man brave, or foolish, enough
to tangle with the huge bouncer of the Jackieboy Saloon.

Nor had Knuckles. Caught with one foot off the ground he
could do nothing to prevent himself reeling backwards. He
smashed down to a table which shattered under his weight and
deposited him in a heap on the ground.

"You shouldn't have done that, cowboy!" said the tubby
man. "Now you've made Knuckles angry."

Which could have been classed as the understatement of the
year. Knuckles had gone past mere anger. He snarled with
rage, foam forming on his lips as he rolled over on to hands
and knees. One hand clamped on a table leg he came to his feet
holding it like a club in his fist. He attacked with a rush as
dangerous as the charge of a long-horn bull.

Not a person in the room spoke as they watched. The big
blond Texan looked strong, but no man had ever stood up to
Knuckles in one of his murderous rages.

With the table leg raised Knuckles came in fast. Mark
watched him, seeing the strength, noticing the slowness.
Knuckles had been a prize-fighter but like most of his kind
fought with brute strength alone, by standing toe-to-toe and
trading blows until one of them could take no more. His
instinct for fighting had become settled into his routine and he
could not believe that any other man fought in a different
manner. So he expected, if indeed he troubled to think about it
all, that Mark would stand there to be hit with the table leg.
Believing this he launched a blow that should have flattened
Mark's head level with his shoulders. Only it did not land.

At the last instant, when most folks watching thought he
had left it too late, Mark sidestepped the rush. The table leg
missed him and shattered to pieces on the floor. Carried forward by his own impetus Knuckles lost his balance once more.
He staggered forward a step and Mark, with a grace and agility a lighter, smaller man might have envied, pivoted around
and threw a punch. The blow, driven with strength, skill and
precision, traveled fast and landed hard. It crashed into and
mangled still more Knuckles's fight-damaged right ear.

Knuckles shot forward, head down and with no control over

his body. The man's close-cropped skull smashed into the bar front and shattered through it. He disappeared behind the bar, knocking the bartender from his feet and preventing him from grabbing up the ten gauge shotgun which lay under the counter for use at such times. With a yell the bartender went down, Knuckles's heavy body on top of him.

A concerted gasp rose from the watching crowd. Everyone expected Knuckles to come roaring through the hole in the bar and stomp the big Texan clear into the floorboards. In this they were to be disappointed for it would be another four hours before Knuckles could move under his own power again.

"I don't like you, you nasty man!" hissed the tubby man from behind Mark. "I don't like you at all!"

The words brought Mark around in a fast turn. He found his aid in handling the matter unnecessary. Even as the tubby man's hand started to lift from his pocket with something metallic glinting in it, the young cowhand took a hand. He rose to one knee, his right fist caught the man in the fat belly and folded him like a closed jack-knife. Then the cowhand came to his feet, the other fist lashed up to catch the tubby man's jaw, jerking him erect and over on to his back. A nickel plated Remington Double Derringer came from the fat man's pocket, left his hand to fly across the room as he fell. The gun looked dainty and fancy enough to have come from the garter of a high-class saloon girl, but that made it no less deadly.

"Freeze!" Mark barked, hearing the rumble of talk from the crowd and facing them with his matched Army Colts in his hands, lined in their general direction.

They all froze for not one member of the crowd failed to notice how fast the guns came out, nor how competently Mark handled them. Apart from the whining and moaning of the tubby man on the floor not a sound came for a long moment.

Mark's nostrils quivered. He could smell a rich perfume which seemed to be vaguely familiar, yet he could not remember for the moment where he last smelled it. This time he could locate the source for the fat shape sprawled on the floor reeked of it. The perfume should mean something, Mark knew. The fat man smelled of the perfume, it rose and hung around him like a cloud.

"Look here, mister," said one of the customers in a conciliatory tone. "We don't know what set Jackieboy there and Knuckles on to the cowhand. Reckon anything between you and him's your affair and he ain't doing nothing much about it. But I got a chance of filling a straight here."

"Go ahead then," replied Mark, holstering his guns. "Only don't blame me if you miss filling it."

The young cowhand had made his feet now. He looked around the room, then said, "We'd best get out of here. Likely somebody's gone for the law."

"Sure," Mark agreed. "What started all this fuss?"

"There you got me. I came in, bought me a drink. Then I asked if there was a chance of taking a riding chore in these parts and the next thing I knew they was both of them on me. The name's Morg Summers."

From his talk Morg hailed from the north country. He looked like a competent cowhand, one who could be relied on to stay loyal to any brand into whose wagon he threw his bedroll.

"I'm Mark Counter," Mark answered as they walked side by side across the room. "Happen you got no other plans I might be able to put a riding chore your way real soon."

They reached the doors and passed forth. From the moment their feet hit the sidewalk both knew they were in trouble. It showed in the shape of the eight men who lounged around in a half circle before the doors. They wore deputy marshal's badges and looked as mean a pack of cut-throats as a man could want to see. Only this looked like the town marshal had extra staff, for Lasalle claimed but eight men worked for Elben and two remained safely hog-tied in the Land Agent's office.

In the center of the group, with a pomaded blond hair, a moustache and goatee beard stood the town marshal himself, looking like a fugitive from a Bill-show. He had a high crowned white Stetson, a fringed buckskin jacket, cavalry style trousers with shining Jefferson boots. A gunbelt supporting a matched brace of ivory handled Remington Beals Army revolvers butt forwards in the holsters. All in all he looked far too well dressed to be honest and much too prosperous for a lawman in a small Texas town.

"What went on inside there?" he asked.

"Enough," Mark replied. "You want to tell that swish to

keep his tame bear chained afore somebody throws lead into it.''

"Don't get flip with me!" Elben snarled. "I'm taking you both to jail on charges of assault and disturbing the peace.''

"I got assaulted and my peace disturbed too," Morg answered. "You going to jail the folks who done it?''

"Shut your mouth!" Elben replied.

"Happen I ever get to be a taxpayer you sure won't get my vote," Morg threatened. "How about it, Mark?''

Mark knew the men wouldn't chance using guns against him unless they were pushed into it. He also knew he could not risk being taken to jail. Any time now the men down in Mallick's office might wriggle their way free, or might be found. Before that happened Freda must be taken safely out of town. Mallick didn't look the kind of man who would let her being a woman stop him from roughing her up or worse. Two against eight were poor odds, but Dusty was on hand and could likely get to them in time to help.

The game was taken out of Mark's hands. A man darted from the saloon, arms clamping around the big Texan from behind. At the same moment the rest jumped into the fray.

While still held from behind by a man who had some strength in his arms, Mark brought up his feet, rammed them into the chests of the deputies who came at him from the front. He thrust out the legs and reeled them backwards. The man holding him staggered, but still retained his grip. To one side Morg Summers proved that he could handle his end in a rough-house even against odds.

A face appeared before Mark, a snarling face surrounded with pomaded hair. Elben moved forward snarling, "You lousy cow-nurses're going to learn not to play rough in my town.''

He moved his fist brutally into Mark's stomach, bringing a gasp of pain for Mark could do nothing to escape the blow. Even as Elben drew back his fist to hit again, Mark's boot lashed up. Fortunately for Elben the kick did not land full force. Had it landed with all Mark's strength the town marshal would not have risen for a long time. Even with the limited power behind it Elben jack-knifed over and collapsed holding his middle and croaking in pain.

With a surge of his muscles Mark flung the man who held

him first to one side then the other. The man lost his hold and went to one side. Mark shot out a fist which sprawled an attacker backwards, backhanded another into the hitching rail. Then they were at him from all sides. He fought back like a devil-possessed fury. This was Mark's element, in a fight against odds, tangling with hard-cases.

By the time Morg Summers went down four of the deputies lay stretched on the ground, one with a nose spread over most of his face and and all carrying marks from two pairs of hard cowhand fists. Sheer weight of numbers got them down in the end. Mark saw Morg go down, staggered one of his attackers and leapt to try and prevent the young cowhand taking a stomping. A man behind Mark drew his revolver and swung it. Mark heard the hiss of the blow and started to try to avoid it. The barrel of the weapon caught him a glancing blow, but one hard enough to drop him to his hands and knees. He stayed there, head spinning, brain unable to send any instructions to his body or coordinate protective movements.

"Get away from him!" Elben snarled, making his feet and looking down at Mark with an expression of almost maniacal rage. He waved back the remaining deputies who were preparing to attack the fallen Mark. "He's mine and I want to see his blood."

Mark heard the voice. It seemed to come from a long way off. The fight had been rough and not all the blows handed out by himself or Morg. He could not shake the pain from him, clear his head enough to protect himself. He did not see Elben coming at him, nor was the marshal more observant. Only one thing mattered to Elben, that he might take revenge on the blood giant who humiliated him before the town. Snarling in fury he drew back his foot for a kick, looking down at Mark. When he got through the big Texan wouldn't look so handsome, nor so high and mighty. Mark knew none of this. He shook his head to try and clear it and wondered why no more blows landed on him as he tried to get up.

In Roylan's store, Dusty heard the girl's excited words. So did the hired gunman, heard them and read their true meaning. He came up with a hand fanning his side, reaching for his gun. "You're not—!" he began.

Dusty wasted no time. Nor did he rely on his guns to stop the man. He came forward and left the floor in a bound, right, foot lashing out into the gunman's face. The man's body slammed backwards into the counter and clung there. Dusty landed on his feet and threw a punch the moment he hit the floor. His right fist shot out, the gunman's head snapped to one side. He went clear over the cracker barrel, landed flat on his back and did not make another move.

Before Roylan could catch his breath, long before he could get over this unexpected turn of events. Dusty faced him, a Colt lined on his chest.

"You go help your pard, mister," Roylan said quickly. "I'll take care of this here unfortunate feller as was supposed to be protecting me. I've got the note from Mallick to cover me."

Without a word Dusty hurled himself from the building, holstering his Colt as he went. He saw the crowd along the street and headed towards it on the run. Roylan caught Freda by the arm as she started to go after dusty.

"Who is he?" he asked, sounding real puzzled. "What happened and what's coming off, Freda, gal. How the hell did he make that kick and down the gunny. Where'd you get the note from?"

"He's Dusty Fog and helping us!" the girl replied as she tore free from his grip and raced after dusty.

She answered two of Roylan's questions, but not the third. Freda did not know of the small Oriental man down in the Rio Hondo. A man thought to be Chinese by the unenlightened majority, but known to be Japanese by his friends. To Dusty Fog alone this man taught the secrets of karate and ju-jitsu fighting. They stood Dusty in good stead and helped him handle bigger men with considerable ease as had the karate flying high kick Dusty used to set up the deputy for a finish in a hurry.

Along the street Elben drew back his foot and made sure of his balance, the better to savor the forthcoming kicking. He heard the thunder of hooves, saw his men scatter and fell back to avoid being trampled by two horses which raced at him. He opened his mouth to bellow curses and his hands dropped towards his sides.

The taller of the riders unshipped from his saddle, landing between Mark and Elben. He stood tall and slim, almost delicate looking. His clothes were Texas cowhand except for the brown coat he wore, its right side stitched back to leave clear the ivory grips of his low tried Army Colt. His face looked pale, studious almost yet the pallor was tan resisting, not one caused by sitting indoors or through ill health. His right hand made a sight defying flicker and the Colt seemed to almost meet it in midair, muzzle lining full on Elben's middle and ending his move almost as soon as it began.

"Back off, *hombre!*" ordered the slim man.

His pard wheeled the big horse between his knees, halting it and facing the deputies. He held a Winchester rifle in his hands, lining it full on them and ending their attempts to draw weapons. In appearance he was as much a Texas cowhand as his pard. Stocky, capable and tough looking, with rusty red colored hair and a face made for grinning. Only he did not grin now, his eyes flashed anger and he looked like he was only waiting for any excuse to throw lead.

"Is Mark all right, Doc?" asked the rusty-haired cowhand.

"He'd best be," replied the slim man called Doc, watching Elben's hands stay clear of the guns as he backed away.

"This's law matter you've cut in on!" Elben snarled, trying a bluff.

It failed by a good country mile.

"Kicking a man when he's down!" Doc growled back. "That's about the way of a yellow cur-dog like you, Mister, happen you've hurt Mark bad you'd best go dig a great big hole, climb in and pull the top on you."

At that same moment Dusty arrived. He came on foot, but he came real fast. Halting before the gun-hung deputies he looked them over. He clearly recognized the two riders for he did not ask how they came into this affair, or even spare them more than a single glance.

"You lousy scum!" Dusty said quietly, his grey eyes lashing the men. "All of you and they whip you down, put half of you in the street."

"Just a minute, you!" Elben snarled, seeing Dusty's lack of inches and getting bolder. "I'm taking all of you in."

"You and how many regiments of Yankee cavalry, loud mouth? asked the rusty haired cowhand. "This here's Dusty Fog and that's Mark Counter you started fussing in with."

That put a different complexion on things. Elben knew the names well enough. From the way the big Texan fought he could most likely be Mark Counter and where Mark Counter was Dusty Fog mostly could be found. He could read no sign of humor in the rusty headed cowhand's face, only deadly serious warning.

Whatever Elben may have thought on the subject his deputies acted like they sure enough believed this small man really was Dusty Fog. They crowded together, those who could, in a scared bunch. One of them indicated the two new arrivals.

"That's Rusty Willis and Doc Leroy of the Wedge!" he whispered in an urgent, warning tone.

This gave the others no comfort. Not only were the two men named prominent as members of the Wedge trail crew, they also had long been known as good friends of Dusty Fog and Mark Counter. The Wedge hired hardy cowhands, men who could handle their end in any man's fight and the names of Rusty Willis and Doc Leroy stood high on the roll of honor of the crew.

Freda arrived, dropping to her knees by Mark, trying to help him to rise. She steadied him with her arm and gasped, "Are you all right, Mark?"

That clinched it. The girl gave any of the bunch who might have doubted them proof that the two Texans were who Rusty Willis claimed them to be.

Slowly Mark forced himself up towards his feet, the girl helping him. He pointed towards where Morg lay groaning. The young cowhand had taken a worse beating than Mark, due mainly to his being less skilled in the fistic arts than the big Texan.

"See to him, gal," he ordered.

Turning Mark walked towards Elben, fists clenched. Dusty caught his arm, held him back as Elben drew away.

"Leave it lie, Mark," he said. "Rusty, fetch that buckboard from down there by the store. Bring the hosses with it. And watch the door, there's one inside who might be on his feet again.

Rusty turned his horse without wondering at Dusty's right to give him orders. On the way to the store he substituted the rifle for his Dance Bros. copy of a Colt Dragoon revolver. He guessed that more than a dispute with the local law enforcement officers caused the trouble here. This town did not need all the number of deputies who had been in the fight.

"I'll take that loud-mouthed fighting pimp now, Dusty," Mark said, loosening his gun as he gave Elben the Texans' most polite name for a Kansas lawman.

"You'll get on your hoss when it comes and ride out," Dusty answered, then turned his attention to Elben's men. "And you bunch'll go down the jail and stay there. If I see one of you between now and leaving town I'll shoot him on sight. Not you though, marshal. You're staying here. Happen any of them have smart ideas you'll be the first one to go."

Kneeling by the groaning cowhand Freda looked down at his bruised and bloody face. She felt helpless, scared, wondering if the young man might be seriously injured. The cowhand called Doc Leroy dropped to his knees by her side and reached out a hand. She watched the slim, boneless looking hands moving gently, touching and gently feeling. Doc Leroy looked up towards Dusty, showing relief.

"Nothing that won't heal in a few days," he said. "Have to ride the wagon for a spell."

By this time Rusty was returning with the buckboard and horses. He had seen the man he took to be owner of the store calmly club down a groaning deputy who tried to rise from by the counter.

Bringing the buckboard to a halt by the party Rusty leapt down, helping Doc get the groaning Morg on to the seat by Freda's side. Morg clung on, then pointing to a pair of dun horses which stood hip-shot at the hitching rail, gasped they were his string.

"Rest easy, *amigo*," drawled Rusty. "I'll hitch them on behind."

Dusty and the others mounted their horses. The small Texan jerked his carbine from the saddleboot and looked down at Elben.

"We're leaving, marshal," he said. "You shout and tell those boys of your'n that the first shot which comes our way brings you a lead backbone. See, you'll be walking ahead of us until we reach the city limits."

"And then we'll go back and tear your lousy lil town apart board by board," Rusty warned.

Freda needed no telling what to do. She started the buckboard moving forward with Mark, gripping his saddlehorn, kept by her side. Elben shouted louder than he had ever managed before, warning his men not to interfere. He spent the walk to the edge of the town sweating and hoping that none of the others wanted his post as town marshal for they would never have a better chance of getting it. All they would need to do was to pull a trigger and he'd be deader than cold pork.

All in all Elben felt relieved when he reached the edge of town and obeyed Dusty's order to toss away his matched guns. He prided himself in those expensive Remingtons, but they could be recovered and cleaned later, whereas he possessed but one life which could not be recovered if lead caught him in the right place.

Not until Dusty's party had passed out of sight did Elben return to the town. He found the owner of the saloon, Jackie-boy Disraeli, nursing a swollen jaw and in a fit of rage.

"What happened out there?" Disraeli screamed, sounding more like a hysterical woman than a dangerous man. "Why didn't you smash those men to a pulp for what they did to Knuckles and me?"

"That was Dusty Fog and Mark Counter, boss," Elben replied, hating having to call the saloonkeeper by such a name, but knowing better than to fail while Knuckles still lived. "They had that Lasalle gal with them and two of the Wedge crew. The girl was in to buy supplies."

Elben's voice shook. On the way back to town an awful thought struck him. He suddenly realized just what a risk he had taken. If his kick had landed on Mark Counter he likely wouldn't be alive now to think about it.

"So Lasalle's girl bought supplies," Disraeli hissed. "Then she must have sold out."

At that moment Roylan arrived with his story about how the deputy had been felled by Dusty Fog who then terrorized him and got away. The storekeeper tossed Mallick's note before Disraeli.

"Freda Lasalle had this and your deputy didn't say who Dusty Fog was," he said. "So I served her."

In this Royland cleared his name before blame could be fixed. He did not fear Disraeli and Mallick, but knew they could ruin him, so didn't aim to give them a chance. They had no proof of what happened in his place and he doubted if the deputy could say anything that might give the lie to his story.

Disraeli headed a rush for Mallick's office where they broke open the door and released an irate Mallick and his men. It took some time before the Land Agent could talk. He slumped in his chair, stiff and sore, glowering at Elben.

"We bring extra men to help handle the town and four cowhands ride all over you," he snarled, after hearing the story. "Elben, you're a— Hell-fire and damnation! They took that map I tore up and threw into the wastepaper-basket."

"I thought you destroyed it," hissed Disraeli. Only he, Mallick and Elben now stood in the office. "Why didn't you?"

"Because I didn't get a chance. They came before I could. Now there's only one thing to do. Get to Lasalle's place and kill every last one of them—and fast!"

CHAPTER EIGHT

The Ysabel Kid Meets
A Gentleman's Gentleman

A SMALL drifting cloud of dust on the horizon down to the south warned the Ysabel Kid he had somebody on his trail. He drew rein on top of a hill and looked along his backtrail. He saw the following rider at a distance where most folks could have made out only a tiny, indistinguishable blob. The Kid not only saw the man, but could tell he had two horses along. This in itself meant nothing for many men took their own string of horses along with them. The direction from which he appeared told a story. He came from the Double K area and the Kid knew few riders would get across without being halted by the hired guns and turned back in their tracks.

"He's after us, old Blackie hoss," drawled the Kid. "Dang my fool Comanche way of telling the truth when I'm questioned politelike. I should remember I'm a paleface, most times, and that as such I can be the biggest danged liar in the world without worrying."

The big white snorted gently, wanting to be moving again. With a grin the Kid started Blackie on his way again.

"Wonder what he wants?" he mused, talking to the horse, but never relaxing his wolf cautious watching of the trail ahead of him. The man was still too far behind to cause any menace. "Must be one of that bunch from this morning and looking for evens. Waal, he can have his chance when he comes closer."

Only the man did not seem to be pushing his horse to close up, nor riding the two mounts in rotation, travelling relay fashion. The kid knew he could make his tracks so difficult that he could delay the man—if he happened to be following the Kid's trail. The Kid told that pair of hired guns back on

Double K where he headed and the following man would not
waste time in tracking, but by riding straight for Bent's Ford
could be on hand when the Kid arrived. With that thought in
mind the Kid decided to continue to Bent's Ford, making sure
he arrived before the other man and so be able to keep a wary
eye on all new arrivals.

The sun was long set when the Kid saw the buildings, stream
and lake known the length of the great inter-state cattle trails
as Bent's Ford. The main house showed lights and even where
he sat the Kid could hear music from the bar-room so he did
not need to worry about disturbing the other guests by his arrival.

Why Bent's Ford had such a name when there appeared to
be nothing of fordable nature has been told elsewhere.* The
place served as a stopping off and watering point for the trail
herds headed north across the Indian Nations. On this night
however no herd bedded down near at hand. There were
horses in the corrals, two big Conestoga wagons standing to
one side, teamless and silent, the normal kind of scene for
Bent's most any night of the week.

The Kid rode steadily down towards the buildings. He could
almost swear the man following him had not managed to get
ahead during the dark hours. For all that he did not leave his
leg-weary white stallion in the corral. The horse stood out
amongst others like a snow-drift and would easily be noticed.
Also Blackie did not take to having strange horses around him
and could be very forceful in his objections.

Using the prerogative of an old friend, the Kid took his
horse to Bent's private stables and found, as he hoped, an
empty stall. He meant to attend to his horse before thinking of
himself. With Blackie cooled down, watered and supplied with
both grain and hay, the Kid left his saddle hanging on the
burro in the corner. He drew the old "yellow boy" from the
saddleboot and headed for the barroom.

Although busily occupied in wiping over a glass with a piece
of cloth, the bartender found time to look up and nod a
greeting to the new arrival.

"Howdy, Kid," he greeted. "Looking for Wes Hardin?"

"He here?"

"By the wall there, playing poker with the boss."

* Told in THE HALF-BREED

The bartender and the Kid exchanged glances and broad grins. The poker games between Wes Hardin, Texas gun-fighter, and Duke Bent, owner of Bent's Ford, were famous along the cattle trails. In serious play and skill the games stood high for both men were past masters at the ancient arts of bet-ting and bluffing known as poker. Yet neither had ever come out of a game more than five or so dollars ahead for they played a five to ten cent limit. This did not affect the way in which they played for they gave each deal enough concentra-tion for a thousand dollar pot.

Before he crossed the room, the Kid looked around. The usual kind of crowd for Bent's Ford looked to be present. A few cowhands who spent the winter up north and were now either headed home or waiting in hope of taking on with another trail drive. Travelling salesmen, flashily dressed, loud-talking, boastful as they waited for stage coaches. A trio of the blue uniformed cavalrymen and a buckskin clad scout shared a table. None of them looked to have just finished a long, hard ride.

"Anybody new in, Charlie?" he asked.

"You're the first since sundown," the bartender answered.

"Check this in for me then," drawled the Kid, passing his rifle to the other man who placed it with the double barrelled ten gauge under the bar counter.

With his weapon out of the way, the Kid crossed the room towards where Bent played poker. He stood for a moment studying Bent's burly build, gambler style clothes and remembering the big man made this place almost single-handed, brought it to its present high standard by hard work and guts. Bent had been a cavalry scout, one of the best. He'd also been a lawman, tough and honest. And Bent was all man in the Kid's eyes.

With his back to the wall in the manner of one of his kind, Wes Hardin, most feared gunfighter in Texas, studied his cards. He was tall, slender, with a dark expressionless face and cold, wolf-savage eyes. Hardin wore the dress of a top-hand with cattle, which he was, he also wore a gunbelt which carried a brace of matched Army Colts in the butt forward holsters of a real fast man with a gun. He was that too.

"I'll raise you!" Bent said, fanning his cards between powerful fingers.

"Will you now?" replied Hardin. "I'm going to see that raise and up it."

The Kid watched all this, knowing the two men were completely oblivious of his presence. He moved around to see Hardin's cards, a grin came to his face and he did something no other man in the room would dare to do.

"Should be ashamed of yourself, Wes," he said, "raising on less'n pair of eights like that."

Slamming down his cards with an exclamation of disgust Hardin thrust back his chair and glared at the Indian-dark boy before him. The customers at nearby tables prepared to head for cover when guns roared forth.

"Hello, Lon," said Hardin, relaxing slightly when he saw who cut in. "What damn fool game you playing, you crazy Comanche. I was all set to bluff Bent clear out of the pot."

"Huh!" granted Bent. "You didn't fool me one lil bit." He raked in the pile of chips and started to count them. "Make it you owe me a dollar fifty, Wes."

"Bet you over counted, like always."

The two men glared at each other. They began a lengthy argument, each man casting reflections on the other's morals and general honesty. Things passed between them, insults rocked back and forwards, which would have seen hands flashing hipwards and the thunder of guns if spoken by a stranger.

Somehow the argument got sidetracked as, alternating between recrimination and personal abuse, they started to argue heatedly about a disputed call in a wild card game some three years before. Just what this had to do with the present disagreement passed the Kid's understanding as neither of the men had held the disputed hand, in fact had not even been in the pot where it came up.

A burst of laughter from the Kid brought an end to the argument and they turned their anger on him, studying him with plain disgust.

"What's amusing you, you danged Comanche?" Hardin growled.

"You pair are," answered the grinning Kid. "I've seen you both lose and win plenty without a word, in high stake games. Yet you're sat here whittle-whanging over who won a measly dollar fifty."

"You wouldn't understand it at all, Kid," Bent answered. "It's all a matter of principles, which same you've got none of."

"Man!" whooped the Kid. "Happen principles make folks act like you pair I sure don't want any."

Hardin's face grew more serious, though only men who knew him as well as the Kid and Bent would have noticed it.

"Where at's Dusty and Mark, Lon?" he asked. "I tried to make Moondog City, when I heard about Cousin Danny."*

"We handled it, Wes."

"Cousin Dusty all right now? He felt strong about that lil brother of his."

"He's over it now."

From the way the Kid spoke both men knew the subject was closed. He did not intend talking about the happenings in the town of Moondog. The sense of loss he felt at the death of Dusty's younger, though not smaller brother, still hung on. He did not offer to tell what happened when Dusty, Mark, Red Blaze and himself came to Moondog. They came to see how Danny Fog handled his duties as a Texas Ranger and had found him beaten to death. Danny Fog died because the town did not dare back him against Sandra Howkins' wolf-pack of hired killers. The Kid did not care to think of the days when he, Dusty and Mark stayed in Moondog and brought an end to the woman's reign of terror.

"Been any sign of the OD Connected herd yet?" asked the Kid, not only changing the subject but also getting down to the urgent business which brought him north.

"Nope, we haven't seen any sign of it," Bent replied. ".You fixing to meet up with it here?"

"Was. Only we got us a mite of fuss down below the Texas line. Might take us a spell to handle it and we don't want Red Blaze coming down trail to help us, or waiting here for us to join up."

Due to having been followed the Kid was more than usually alert and watchful. So he saw the man who entered the saloon and stood just inside the doors, looking around. One glance told the Kid this man had not been on his trail, for the trailer had been a westerner and the new arrival anything but that.

He stood maybe five foot eight, slim and erect. His sober

* Told in A TOWN CALLED YELLOWDOG

black suit was well pressed and tidy, his shirt white and his tie of eastern pattern and sober hue. Though his head had lost some of its hair and his face looked parchment-like, expressionless, he carried himself with quiet dignity as he crossed towards where Bent sat at the table. Halting by the table the newcomer coughed discreetly to attract attention to himself.

"Has Sir James' man arrived to guide us to his residence, landlord?" he asked in a strange sounding accent.

"Nope," Bent answered, having grown used to being addressed as landlord by this sober looking dude. "Did you pass anybody on the way north, Lon?"

"Nary a soul," replied the Kid. "You all expecting somebody, friend?"

Swivelling an eye in the Kid's direction, the man looked him over from head to toe. The Kid had ridden hard all day and his black clothes did not look their best, but he reckoned that to be his own concern. To the Kid it seemed this pasty-faced dude did not approve of him or his trail-dirty appearance. This annoyed the Kid, never a man to allow a dude to take liberties with him.

Bent knew this and cut in hurriedly, saying, "Mr. Weems here's expecting one of the Double K to come and guide him and his folks down to the spread."

At first Bent had not taken to Weems. Weems came down from the north with two big Conestoga wagons, each well loaded, but drawn by good horses of a type rarely seen in the west, great heavy legged and powerful creatures which Weems called shire horses. The two wagons had been driven by a pair of gaunt men dressed in a style Bent had never seen before. Two women rode in the wagons and, strangely to western eyes, they did not ride together. Bent suggested that the men shared a room and the two women another. The suggestion was greeted with horror by all concerned, the two drivers insisting it wouldn't be proper to share a room with Mr. Weems and the pretty, snub-nosed, poorly dressed girl stated firmly she could not possibly use the same room as Miss Trumble.

It took Bent a short time to understand the social standing so firmly ingrained in these English travellers. They did not live by the same standards as the men of the West. To the girl, Weems called her a 'tween maid, it was unthinkable that she should room with so exalted a person as Miss Trumble who appeared to be a housekeeper of some kind. So he arranged for the girl to use a small room while Miss Trumble and Weems took two of his expensive guest rooms and the two men insisted on spending the night in the wagons.

"You-all work for Keller, mister?" asked the Kid, his voice sounding Comanche-mean.

"I am *Sir James* Keller's man," replied Weems haughtily and laying great emphasis on the third and fourth words.

"Never took you for a gal!" answered the Kid, getting more riled at the thought of a dude trying to make a fool of him.

Once more Bent intervened in the interests of peace and quiet. "Mr. Weems is a valet, Lon," he said.

"A valley?" asked the Kid, sounding puzzled and wondering if Bent was joining in some kind of a joke.

"V-a-l-e-t, not v-a-l-l-e-y," Bent explained.

"A gentleman's gentlemen," Weems went on, as if that would clear up any doubts the Kid still held.

"Like Tommy Okasi is to Uncle Devil," Hardin put in, helping to clarify the duties of a valet in a manner the Kid understood.

"Never heard ole Tommy called anything as fancy as a valet," drawled the Kid although he knew now what Weems did for his living.

"There's not likely to be anybody up here today," Bent told Weems. "If your boss hasn't anybody here in the morning you could send a telegraph message to Barlock and let him know you've arrived here. Or you could see if there's anybody going down trail who'll act as a guide. But you won't be able to start until the morning either way."

"Thank you, I yield to your greater knowledge."

With that Weems turned and walked towards the bar. Bent looked down at the cards, then raised his eyes to the Kid's face. The struggle between possible financial gains at poker and his keenness at quartet singing warred for a moment and music won out.

"Say, Lon," he said. "Let's see if we can get up a quartet and have us some singing."

Always when the Kid visited Bent's Ford on his way north or south, Bent expected a session of quartet harmony. He possessed a powerful, rolling bass and enjoyed throwing it into the melody, backing the other singers. The Kid stood high on Bent's list of tenors and the Kid was always willing to oblige. Knowing Dusty did not expect him to return before morning, the Kid could relax and enjoy quartet singing in good company.

"Let's go and find us some more singers," drawled the Kid.

"Got us a baritone," Bent replied. "Whiskey drummer over there. Now all we want is another tenor. How about you, Wes?"

"Never took to singing since pappy used to make me get in that fancy lil suit and go into the choir back home."

"I'll get around and ask, Lon," Bent said, as Wes Hardin refused to be drawn into the quartet.

The Kid and Hardin headed for the bar while Bent made a round of the room looking for a second tenor without which no decent quartet could exist. The two Texans took beer, further along the bar Weems leaned with a schooner of beer in his hand looking off into space and speaking with nobody.

"Not another tenor in the place," said Bent in a disappointed tone, joining the other two at the bar.

His words carried to Weems who walked towards them.

"I suppose there is no chance of getting started for the master's residence tonight?" he said.

"Nope, none at all," Bent answered.

"Then may I join your quartet?"

The other men showed their surprise for none of them thought Weems to be a likely candidate for joining in a quartet.

"You?" asked the Kid.

"One sings occasionally," replied Weems calmly. "I recollect the time Sir James' butler and I formed a quartet with the head keeper and head groom. Of course they weren't in our class, but we felt the conventions could be waived at such a time. Without boasting, we made a pretty fair quartet."

The meaning of Weems' words went clear over the heads of his listeners. Not one of them understood the strict hierarchy of servants in upper-class households. Nor were they greatly concerned with such things as conventions, being more interested in getting buckled down to some singing.

One problem might present itself, the choice of songs.

Weems could hardly be expected to know old range favorites.

"Shall we make a start with *Barbara Allen*?" asked Weems.

"Take the lead, friend," replied the Kid.

It took them but the first verse of the old song to know Weems could handle his part and was no mean tenor in his own right. The room fell silent as the customers settled back to listen to real good singing.

After four songs, all well put over and with Weems showing he could lend a hand at carrying a melody even if he did not know the words of the tune, Bent called for liquid refreshment. This gave the Kid a chance to talk to Weems and to try to learn more about Sir James Keller.

"What sort of feller's your boss, friend?" he asked.

"Sir James?" replied Weems. "A gentleman and a sportsman. My family has served his for the past six generations."

"Why'd he come out here?"

"I never asked."

The Kid grinned, warming to Weems. If anybody had questioned him about some of Dusty, or Ole Devil's business he would have made the same reply, in much the same tone. Clearly Weems felt the same loyalty to his boss as a cowhand did to the outfit for which he rode. However the Kid hoped to try and learn if Keller knew what went on around and about his spread.

"Maybe he reckons to make a fortune out here," drawled Wes Hardin.

"We already have a fortune," sniffed Weems, just a trifle pompously. "The master felt we might have a better chance of development out here. After all there is so little scope left in England these days. The whole country's going to the dogs. Why shortly before we sailed a junior footman at Lord Granderville's, in *my* presence, addressed the butler without calling him mister."

To Weems this clearly amounted to the depths of decadence, a sign of the general rottenness of the times. To the listening men it sounded incomprehensible. If a Texan called a man mister after being introduced it meant he did not like the man and wanted no part of him.

Bent took up the questioning and Weems, with the mellowing influence of a couple of beers, talked of the life he had in England. He might have been discussing the habits of creatures from another planet as he described the strict social distinctions between servants. It now became clear to Bent why a between-stairs maid did not consider herself good enough to share a room with so important a person as a housekeeper. The term brought grins to Texas faces. In their world a house did not mean a home and housekeeper sounded like a fancy title for the madam of a brothel. Weems broke in to a delighted chuckle as the Kid mentioned this, trying to picture the puritanical Miss Trumble in such a capacity. He talked on but there was no snobbish feeling in his words. To him it stood as a way of life, one with a code as rigid as that which ruled the lives of cowhands in their loyalty to their brand.

During the talking, even though absorbed by Weems' descriptive powers, the Kid stayed alert. He saw the stocky man who entered the bar room and stood just inside looking around with watchful eyes. For an instant he looked at the Kid, then his eyes passed on, but the Kid had noticed just a hint of recognition in them. The Kid studied the newcomer, noted his dandy but travel-stained clothes, the low hanging Tranter revolver from the butt of which a right hand never strayed. The man looked like a tough hired killer, one of the better class than the pair he'd run across on Double K, or the group he helped chase from Lasalle's, but one of their breed.

Possibly the man might be a guide come to take Weems and his party to the ranch. His next actions proved this to be wrong. The man did not cross to the bar and ask for information about the Weems' party. He sat with his back to the wall and close to the door, and ordered a drink from a passing waiter. Which same meant if he came from the Double K it was not to meet Weems, but to follow the Kid.

"Let's have another song," suggested Bent, getting in another round of beers. "Give us the *Rosemay-Jo Lament*, Lon."

"Why sure," agreed the Kid. "Soon's I've been out back."

Shoving away from the bar, the Kid headed across the room and out of the door. He gave no sign of knowing the man might be after him, but sensed eyes on him as he left the

building. Two horses which had not been there when he
entered, stood at the hitching rail. That meant he guessed
right, the man was the same who followed him north.

For some moments after the Kid's departure Dune sat at the
table and waited. Then he emptied his glass in one swallow,
rose and walked through the doors into the night.

The night lay under the light of a waning moon, but he
could see well enough for his purpose. He glanced at the two
horses, they had brought him from the Double K although he
did not travel at speed. He might have caught up with the Kid
on the range but did not fancy taking such a chance. He had
ridden steadily, keeping reserve energy for a hurried departure. Clearly the Kid had friends in the bar-room and they
were not going to take kindly finding him murdered.

With this thought in mind Dune led the two horses to the
side of the main building and left them. Then he walked
around behind the building, making for the long, three-hole
men's backhouse which lay some distance away.

To discourage his guests from staying inside too long, to the
discomfort of other guests, Bent had three-quarter length
doors on each compartment of the backhouse. This left part
of the top and bottom open and tended to make the occupants
take only such time as was necessary.

Only one compartment of the backhouse appeared to be in
use. Dune saw this and could tell that it held the Ysabel Kid,
for a gunbelt hung over the top of the door, a white handled
bowie knife strapped to it.

Dune looked around him carefully as he drew his Tranter
revolver. Apart from a small bush some twenty feet away he
could see nothing and even the bush was nothing to disturb
him. He did not aim to match up with the Kid in a fair fight
and he had a good chance of avoiding the need to.

Taking aim Dune threw his first bullet into the door. He
knew that the .44 bullets would make light work of smashing
through the planks at that range. Twice more he aimed and
fired, taking only enough time to re-aim and place the bullets a
few inches apart, so they would fan across the interior and
catch the Kid as he sat on the hole.

No sound came from the compartment. Nothing at all.
Dune realized this as he triggered off his third shot. Realized it

and the implication behind the silence. Even had his first bullet struck and killed the Kid there should have been some noise, if only his death throes.

"Finished?" asked a voice from his left.

Dune swung around, trying to turn the Tranter. The Kid's black-dressed shape loomed up from behind the bush Dune had dismissed as being too small to hide even a child. His gunbelt might hang over the backhouse door and show the hilt of the bowie knife as bait for a trap—but the old Dragoon was in his hand.

With a snarled curse Dune tried to line his gun. The Tranter never saw the day when its butt lent itself to fast instinctive alignment and Dune had time for nothing else. He fired, the bullet missed the Kid although it came close enough to stir his shirt sleeve. With a roar like a cannon the old Dragoon bloomed out a reply, flame stabbing towards Dune.

The Kid shot the only way he dare. For an instant kill. His round, soft lead .44 ball caught Dune just over the left eyebrow at the front and burst in a shower of bone splinters and brains out at the back of the head. Such was the striking power of the old gun that Dune went over backwards, thrown from his feet. The Tranter fell from a lifeless hand even before his body hit the ground.

Shouts sounded from the main building. Windows of the upper floor rooms opened and people looked out. Then Bent and Wes Hardin, both holding weapons, burst into sight, racing towards the Kid. Other occupants of the bar-room came next including some of the staff carrying lanterns.

"What happened?" Bent asked the Kid who stood strapping on his gunbelt once more.

"Take a look. That *hombre* sure messed up your backhouse door."

Taking a lantern from a waiter, Wes Hardin came forward and let the light play on the door. His eyes took in the three holes. From their height and position he could guess at what would have happened had the Kid been sitting inside.

"Who was he, Lon?" asked Bent, for he handled law enforcement in that section of the Indian Nations.

"Never saw him afore, until he walked into your place tonight. Any of these folks know him?"

Bent allowed the onlookers to move forward, but none of them could say who the dead man might be. Dune's face, apart from the hole over his eye, was not marked even though the back of his head proved to be a hideous mess when exposed to view.

The two horses did not help either, one came from a south Texas ranch, by its brand; the other from a spread which specialized in the breeding and selling of saddle stock.

"Nothing in his pockets to identify him," Bent stated, making a check. "Sure you don't know him, Lon?"

"Nope."

Bent threw a look at the Kid, knowing the sound of his voice. When that note crept into the Kid's voice it was no use asking him questions. So Bent shrugged and turned to order his men to remove the body.

The Kid found Weems at his side. They watched men carrying away the body headed for the stables where it could be left until morning when it would be buried.

"You killed him," said the valet, his face looking ashen pale.

Tapping the door by the line of bullet holes, the Kid nodded. "I reckon I did. He wasn't in this much of a hurry to get in and even if he had been there's two more empty holes."

"And you didn't know him?"

"Nope. He could have mistaken me for somebody else. Say, I'm headed down trail in the morning. Happen you feel like it I'll show you to Double K."

Weems gave the matter some thought. This soft-talking, innocent looking young man had just killed a fellow human being. True the other man appeared to have given good cause for the action, but in England people did not treat killing so lightly. However Weems had his duty to his master. He must get the two wagon loads of furniture and property to the house as soon as possible. He decided to take a chance. Like his master, Weems had been escorted from Kansas by cavalrymen from Fort Dodge, their colonel being a friend of Sir James. However Weems's escort were ordered to return at Bent's Ford where a guide from the ranch would be waiting. The guide had not arrived and Weems wished for no more delay. Who knew what a position Sir James might find himself in, alone, without the services of a good valet in the raw, primitive west?''

"I'll be pleased to have you along," he said.

"We'll pull out at sun-up then," replied the Kid. "Now I'd best get back inside, likely Duke Brent'll want to see me some more about that *hombre* I had to kill.''

CHAPTER NINE

Keep Back Or I'll Kill You

DUSTY Fog turned in his saddle and looked back along the trail to Barlock. What he saw satisfied him and he slid the Winchester carbine back into its saddle-boot.

"They're not following us," he remarked.

Rusty Willis scoffed at the thought. "Course not. They know I'm along."

"You don't smell that bad yet," grunted Mark. "How you feeling, Morg?"

The young cowhand from the north country managed a wry grin and tried to ease his aching body on the buckboard seat. he didnt want the men, all well known members of his trade, to think him a whiner.

"Like one time a hoss throwed me off then walked over me. T'aint nothing but half a dozen or so broken ribs, all us Montana boys are tough."

This brought howls of derision from the others. Freda watched them and smiled, wondering if cowhands ever grew up so old as to take life seriously. She also gave a sideways look at Morg Summers; he seemed capable and honest, not bad looking either if it came to a point.

"Say Freda, gal," Mark went on. "Morg here's looking for a riding chore and you're looking for a hand or so. Must be fate in it somewhere."

"I'd have to be able to call him something more than just Morg," she replied.

"Why?" grinned Mark, watching the flush which crept to the girl's cheeks. "All right. This's Morgan Summers, from Montana, 'though why he'd boast about that I sure don't know. Morg, get acquainted with Freda Lasalle; my pard

Dusty Fog; and this pair are from the Wedge, but don't hold it again 'em. They answer to Rusty Willis and Doc Leroy and if you can't sort out which's which you north country hands are even less smart than I allow you are.''

"Rusty Willis's the best looking one," Rusty prompted.

"Howdy Rusty," Morg replied, looking at Doc. "I'd recognize you from your pard's description."

All in all Morg allowed he had made the right impression on the others. He wanted to make a good impression on them all —especially the girl who sat so close besides him and handled the ribbons of the buckboard so competently.

"I think we can manage to hire you," Freda stated, wondering if her father would agree, then she looked towards Mark in a coldly accusing manner. "What started the trouble in town?"

Leaving Mark to explain, or to keep the girl occupied, for his explanation in the first place bore little resemblance to the truth, Dusty turned his attention to the two Wedge hands. He had not seen them in a couple of years, but they looked little different. Doc still looked as studious and frail as ever, and most likely could still handle his gun with the old speed and skill. Rusty clung to his old Dance Brothers revolver, a Confederate .44 calibre copy of the Dragoon Colt and he did not look any less reliable for that.

"Where at's the herd?" Dusty asked.

"Down trail a piece," replied Doc. "Rusty and me cut on ahead to Barlock to pick up some makings. You look like you've found some fuss up here, Dusty."

"Man'd say you were right at that," Dusty agreed.

Then he told the story of their visit to Lasalle's and what came out of it. He saw the change in his friends' faces as he spoke of that wire across the narrows and Mallick's threat that no trial herd would go through his land. They did not offer any comment until he finished then Rusty let out a low exclamation, obscene but to the point.

"Clay Allison's about two days behind us and to the southwest," he went on. "Johnny saw him on a swing around the herd. There'll surely be all hell on when old Clay hears about that wire."

Doc nodded his agreement and Dusty saw nothing to argue about in it. They all knew Clay Allison, a Texas rancher and one of the real fast guns in his own right. If he arrived and found his trail blocked he would have a real good answer, roaring guns.

A thought hit Doc Leroy and he reined in his horse, looking at Dusty.

"If those yahoos from the Double K hit Lasalle's they likely went for the other spreads at the same time."

An angry grunt left Dusty's lips. He should have thought of that in the first place. However he did not waste time in futile self-recrimination, or in discussing the chance of the Double K making visits.

He rode forward to the buckboard and interrupted Mark's description of how he and Morg were saving the virtue of a beautiful salloongirl when the marshal's bunch jumped them, with Morg protesting his innocence in the matter of rescuing beautiful saloongirls.

"Reckon you can get this pair of invalids back to your place without us along, Freda?" he asked.

"I reckon I can. If lies were health Mark's sure well enough. You're not going back to Barlock, are you?"

"Nope," Dusty answered. "So don't get all hot and bothered. Doc's just reminded me of something I should've thought of sooner."

"What's that?" she asked.

"The same thing that bunch tried at your place might've been done to your neighbors, only more so."

Freda gave a low gasp for she had not thought of the possibility either. She instantly became practical and helpful, pointing off across the range roughly in the direction of the Gibbs' place, then how they would be able to find the Jones' house.

"Want me along, Dusty?" Mark asked.

"Not this time, *amigo*," replied Dusty. "Three of us should be enough and I'd like somebody on hand at Freda's in case that bunch comes back."

Although he would have much rather rode with Dusty, Mark knew his small pard call the game right. Not only would an extra pair of hands give strength to the Lasalle house if an attack came, but Mark himself needed to get off his horse and rest. That fight in town had taken plenty out of him, enough to make him more of a liability than an asset in the sort of conditions Dusty, Doc and Rusty might be running into.

Knowing hired gunmen, Mark guessed Tring would be smarting under the indignity of failure and in being fanned off the Lasalle place by a load of bird shot. He might easily gather his bunch and make for the Lasalle house to avenge himself and Mark wanted to be on hand when he came.

So Mark stayed with the buckboard while Dusty swung off at a tangent, riding with his two good friends of the Wedge. Mark grinned at the girl's worried face and said, "Waal, there was ole Morg, with this beautiful blonde haired gal on his lap and all—"

"You danged white-topped pirate!" wailed Morg. "Whyn't you tell the truth for once in your life?"

"All right," grinned Mark. "She wasn't beautiful, She was about two hundred pounds weight, had seven double chins—"

"Let's ignore him, Morg," suggested Freda, interrupting Mark's flow of descriptive untruth. "You tell me what happened."

Which brought her no nearer to knowing the truth for Morg reversed the story Mark told, putting Mark in his place in every detail.

"That I can well believe," Freda remarked at the end. "Now—and I want to remind all and sundry that I am the sole cook at home—how about telling me what really happened."

"A wise man once told me never to argue with the cook," Mark drawled. "It all started when I saw Morg getting abused by that Jackieboy saloon bunch."

This time Freda heard the true story. She felt grateful to Mark for having saved Morg Summers and almost wished she had not slapped Mark's face back in town.

For a time after leaving the buckboard Dusty and the other two rode in silence. Beyond expressing their regrets at the death of Dusty's brother neither Doc nor Rusty made any other reference to the happenings in Moondog. They were all good friends with past dangers shared, so did not need to go into words to show their true feelings. Dusty turned the talk to the wire and the other two growled their anger. All agreed on one thing. The fence must go. Rusty and Doc were all for war, although Doc, more given to thinking of causes and effects than his *amigo* saw how a wire cutting war might affect the inhabitants of the area.

"I can't see Clay Allison sitting back peaceable and talking,

Dusty," drawled Rusty Willis, "even if Stone will."

"I'm going to talk to them both," Dusty answered. "I'll ride down trail in the morning and meet up with Clay. He'll stand firm maybe, if I explain things to him."

"What sort of things?" Rusty asked.

"Like what'll happen to these folks up here happen a war starts over their land."

"That'd tangle their lines for sure," agreed Doc Leroy. "It'd be them who go to the wall if the trail herds were held up and grazed their land out, to say nothing of the fighting that'd be going on."

Then Rusty saw it. He had seen an area blasted wide open by a range war between two big outfits. There were three smaller places around the scene of the war and at the end of it all lay empty and deserted, the owners either killed or run out by the opposing factions.

They rode across the range and struck a track made by wagon wheel ruts which, according to Freda's directions, ought to lead to the Gibbs' spread. After following the tracks for a couple of miles they topped a rim and looked down.

"You were right, Doc," Dusty said quietly and grimly. "Double K didn't just call on Lasalle."

Neither Doc nor Rusty made any reply to this, Rusty growled a low, barely audible string of curses, but Doc said nothing. His long, slim fingers drummed on his saddle horn as his eyes took in the scene below.

The corral fence had been smashed down. The house's front door hung on its lower hinges, the top having been smashed open. Not a single pane of glass remained unbroken at the windows. Nor did the destruction end with the corral and main house. The outbuilding doors had been burst in, their walls battered into gaping holes. Not a living thing showed about the place. Several dead chickens lay before the house and the body of a big bluetick hound sprawled stiff and still by the corral fence.

"Let's go!" Dusty growled and started his horse forward.

Slowly they rode down the slope towards the house. Not one of them spoke as they studied the wreck of a well-kept spread and a neat, clean house.

"Keep away!" screamed a woman's voice from the house. "Keep back of I'll kill you!"

Hysteria filled the woman's voice, but the three men did not stop. They rode slowly on and halted their horses by the corral. Dusty started to swing down from his saddle when Rusty's voice, tense and warning, stopped him.

"Dusty! The door! Turn slow and easy!"

Turning his head Dusty looked towards the broken door of the house. He found himself looking at the barrels of a ten gauge shotgun. Behind the shotgun, holding it waist high but aimed at them, stood a pretty, plump, red-haired woman. Slowly Dusty swung down from his saddle and took a step forward, hands well clear of his sides, eyes never leaving her face.

She would have been a happy woman, full of the joys of life, friendly and kind, most times. Now her face bore marks of the strain she was under and he eyes were red rimmed, swollen with tears. She came through the door, a smallish woman wearing an old gingham dress and with a face which told that she had been through living hell that day.

"Keep back!" she repeated. "Haven't you done enough? My husband isn't even conscious yet! He can't do anything!"

"Easy, ma'am," replied Dusty, watching her all the time and stepping closer. "We're not from the Double K."

He might never have spoken for all the effect his words had on her. it did not even appear that the woman heard his words. She brought up the shotgun a trifle and Doc bit down a warning shout just in time.

"Watch her, Dusty!" he warned in a voice which sounded nearer a whisper than a shout. "One wrong move and you'll be picking buckshot out of your back teeth. She's scared loco and'd do it without even knowing."

Slowly as a snail crossing a leaf, Dusty moved forward. He did not for an instant take his eyes from the woman's face, trying to hold her attention on him. So far she had not pressed the shotgun's trigger but one fast move could cause her forefinger to close and send the weapon's deadly charge into him. Despite his earlier scoffing Dusty knew even a charge of birdshot at that range would be more than lethal and would blow a hole like a cannon's bore in him. One quick move, one sudden sound even, might cause her to press the trigger.

It was as deadly and dangerous a situation as Dusty had ever been in. Perhaps the most dangerous. If this had been a man bad mean and set on killing, Dusty could have handled things differently. Only this was no man, but a terrified woman driven to the verge of madness, hysterical and not responsible for her actions.

Perhaps Doc Leroy knew the danger better than Rusty, than Dusty even. For a time, before circumstances sent him home to Texas and to become a cowhand working for Stone Hart's Wedge, Doc read medicine in an eastern college. He did not complete the course but spent every spare minute when in town working with the local medicine man, learning all he could. On the trail he handled the doctoring chores which fell to the cook in most cases. He would take care of injuries, splint and care for broken limbs, diagnose various illnesses and produce their cures, within the limitations of his medical supplies. He probably knew more about the extraction of bullets than most eastern doctors ever learned. On two occasions, when driven to it by the force of circumstances, he delivered babies. So Doc had knowledge of the effect of hysteria. He knew the full danger of Dusty going towards the woman and he felt more scared than he had ever been in his life.

Still moving slowly Dusty made his way towards the woman, edging to the right with the barrels of the gun following him like iron filings after a magnet. He knew his friends were now clear of the shotgun's charge and there only remained the problem of getting the weapon away from her without taking its charge full in his belly. For the first time he looked down at the gun, seeing that the right side hammer only had been cocked back, the left lying safe and down.

An inch at a time, moving with the same slowness which covered all his moves since dismounting, Dusty's right hand went up, gripped the brim of his Stetson and removed it. He was close to the woman, but not close enough to chance a straight grab, not while her finger rested on the trigger. However the gun aimed at him, his friends were in the clear. He had brought them into this mess and must get them out of it without injury if possible. That was the way Dusty Fog thought and acted.

"Just take it easy, ma'am," he said, keeping his voice gentle and fighting to hold the tension out of it. His eyes were on her face once more. "Afore you can shoot you'll have to cock back the hammers."

The woman's eyes dropped towards the breech of her shotgun. For an instant her finger relaxed on the trigger. Instantly Dusty slapped his hat around, knocking the shotgun's barrels to the right while he made a fast side step to the left. For all that it was close, very close. The gun bellowed, he felt the hot muzzle blast and the hot rush of air and burnt powder stirred his shirt, but the lethal load, not yet spread on leaving the barrel, missed him.

Jumping forward Dusty grabbed the shotgun by its barrels and dragged forward at it. The woman gave a scream of terror, she tried to fumble back the second hammer but Dusty plucked the shotgun from her hands. She stood for a moment, staring at Dusty, while Doc and Rusty came out of their saddles and the mount Dusty borrowed from Lasalle took off for home on the run.

"Catch my saddle, Rusty!" Dusty yelled, giving the old range request for aid; for while the horse a cowhand rode mostly belonged to the ranch's remuda it carried his more precious and vital item of personal property, his saddle.

The words seemed to shake the woman out of her paralysis. With a scream she flung herself at Dusty, coming all teeth and fingernails, a wild-cat ready to use primeval fighting equipment to defend her home and husband. Dusty did not dare take a chance. He caught her by the wrists, holding her as she struggled with almost super-human strength, feet lashing out and arms fighting against his grip. He saw Rusty take off after his departing horse and felt relieved. Nothing in the west caused so much anxiety as a riderless, saddled horse. Dusty knew Mark would be worried if his mount came back to Lasalle's empty. He did not want his big *amigo* coming looking for him and leaving the Lasalle house with only a small guard.

For a moment the woman struggled, until Doc caught her by the arms from behind and held her. Then she seemed to collapse into herself. The shotgun, thrown to one side by Dusty when he found need to prevent her scratching his eyes out, lay on the ground but she did not look at it. Instead she lifted dull, lifeless eyes to his face and spoke in a strangled voice.

"All right. Do what you like with me, but leave my husband alone."

Dusty and Doc released her, but Dusty took up the shotgun and removed its percussion cap to make sure the weapon could

not be turned against him. Then he stood with his back to the
two, allowing the tension to ooze from him. In his time as a
lawman Dusty had found cause to use a shotgun on a man, it
was not a pretty sight. A man did not just shake off, and laugh
at it as being nothing, almost winding up the same way.

Knowing how Dusty must feel, Doc gently turned the
woman to face him. "Now easy there, ma'am," he said.
"We're not from the Double K."

"Freda Lasalle sent us over," Dusty went on, his voice
sounding just a little shaky still, and not turning around.

At that moment Doc threw a look at the partly open door of
the house. What he saw brought an angry growl for his throat
and sent him running for the house. Dusty turned and followed, seeing what Doc saw and forgetting his personal feelings in the urgency of the matter. The woman turned, watching them, looking as if all her will had been drained out of her.
Then she heard hooves and turned to see Rusty riding back,
leading the Lasalle's horse. He swung down from the saddle,
left his horse standing with its reins dangling and the runaway
fastened to the saddlehorn. Coming towards the woman he
threw a glance at the stiff body of the bluetick hound.

"Nobody but a stinking Yankee'd shoot a good dawg like
that'n," he said in a tone that boded ill for the man who shot
the dog if Rusty ever laid hands on him. "Where'd I find a
spade, ma'am? I'll tend to burying him."

He got no reply, for the woman turned on her heels and fled
to the house, Rusty did not follow, but headed for the damaged barn to see if he could find a shovel.

Dusty and Doc were already in the house. The building,
made on the same lines as Lasalle's home, had once been just
as neat, tidy and pleasant. Now the front room looked as if a
whirlwind had passed through it. The table had been thrown
over, chairs broken, the sofa's covers slashed open to expose
springs and stuffing. The cupboards were shattered and
broken, crockery lying in pieces on the floor. Just inside the
door, face down, head resting on a pillow lay the woman's
husband, a tall, powerful looking man of middle-age. His
back carried marks left by the lash of a blacksnake whip.

"Don't touch him!" gasped the woman, entering the room
just as Doc went to his knees by the man.

"Get me some hot water, ma'am," Doc answered gently.

"Happen they've left you anything to heat it in. And I'll want some clean white cloth. I've got to get that shirt off and tend to his back."

At last the woman seemed to realize that her visitors meant her no harm. She made an effort, then led Dusty to the kitchen. It appeared the Double K restricted their efforts to the out-buildings and the front room for the neat kitchen remained intact and she had already been heating water when they rode up.

"What happened, ma'am?" Dusty asked, leading the woman from the room as soon as she gave Doc the water and cloth. Doc was never too amiable when handling a medical or surgical chore and it paid to steer well clear of him at such times.

"Some of the Double K men came to see us early on. They told us to sell out and leave. Said they would be back after they saw the Joneses. Later on they came back. Ralph told them he didn't aim to quit and they jumped him. Sam tried to help, but one of them shot him down. They lashed Ralph to the corral and whipped him, while one of them held me, made me watch. Then they wrecked everything they could and rode away. They said they'd be back tomorrow. I thought you—I thought—Oh lord! I nearly k-killed you!"

"You were scared, ma'am," Dusty answered. "You couldn't know."

The sound of digging brought her attention from Dusty. She looked to where Rusty Willis, who at normal times wouldn't have thought of touching the blister end of a spade, dug a grave for the dog.

Then she turned and started to cry, the sobs ripping from her, tears pouring down her cheeks in a steady flow. The anguish she must have held bottled up inside while she tried to do something for her husband and about the wreck of her home, boiled out of her. She knew herself to be safe and in good hands. Now she could be a woman and cry out her misery.

Dusty let her get on with it, knowing she would be better once the crying ended. He waited by her side and at last she dried her eyes, turning to him once more and showing she had full control of herself.

"I should help your friend. I was a nurse for a time in the

War. After the men rode away I managed to get Ralph inside the house. I had laudanum in the medicine chest, they hadn't touched it. I gave Ralph some to ease the pain. I didn't know what to do for the best. Can your friend do anything for my husband?"

"Reckon he can, ma'am? There was a time when a trail hand for the Wedge took sick, like to die. Ole Doc there, he went to work and operated with a bowie knife and a bottle of whisky. He saved that hand's life. Yea, I reckon he can handle your husband's hurts all right."

At that moment they heard the sound of hooves. Rusty dropped the spade and fetched out his Dance. Dusty turned, hands ready to bring out the matched Colts. He knew only one horse approached but prepared to tell the woman to head for the house. It didn't seem likely that Double K would send one man to visit the ranch, but one of the hired guns might have the idea that a woman left alone and in a state of terror would be easy meat.

"Don't shoot!" Joyce Gibbs gasped, seeing and recognizing the rider. "It's Yance. He works for Pop Jones."

Riding at a fast trot the grizzled cowhand came towards the others. He halted his horse and threw a glance at Dusty and Rusty, then relaxed. Neither were the kind Double K hired.

"See they been here, too," he said in an angry tone. "They treat you folks bad, Mrs. Gibbs?"

"Ralph's hurt," she replied. "These gents came by and lent a hand. Have they been to your place?"

"Came in on their way through here. Told Pop to sell out and go. He allows to do it. Him and Maw's getting too old for fussing with that bunch. I'd've started shooting, but Maw said no."

"When do they have to leave by, friend?" Dusty asked, stepping by Joyce.

"Double K allow to come in tomorrow and make sure we're ready to up stakes and pull out."

Studying Dusty, the cowhand did not see a small, insignificant man, he saw a master of their trade, a tophand more than normally competent with the matched brace of guns he wore. Yance did not know from where Dusty and Rusty came, but he knew they looked like the kind of men who could handle the Double K bunch. He hoped they would stay on and help the Gibbs family who were real nice folks and deserved better than to be driven out from their homes. Yance was more than willing to listen to any words of wisdom the small Texan might hand out.

"You head back to your spread," Dusty told him. "I'll try and get a couple or so hands over to you in the morning. If they haven't made it by ten o'clock tell your boss to upstakes and head for Lasalle's. Don't stand and fight."

"You at Lasalle's?" Yance asked.

"Sure."

"I'll tell Pop. Only I sure hope that you-all can get the men to us. I'd like to tie into Double K with some good men at my back."

He wasted no more time in talk. Turning his horse he headed for his home spread, but he rode in a more jaunty manner. Joyce saw this and wondered who the small man might be.

"Who are you?" she asked, then her face flushed red for such a question was never asked in polite western society.

For once Dusty took no offense at the words. He introduced himself and Rusty telling her who Doc was. Then he kept her talking while Rusty finished the grave-digging and buried the dog.

"They broke a tea set my mother gave me for my wedding!"she said suddenly, recalling something. Tears glistened in her eyes as she said the words and she clenched her fists, trying to avoid breaking down once more for the reaction still hung over her.

"One thing I promise, ma'am," Dusty replied. "The man responsible for this lot here's going to pay for it."

CHAPTER TEN

The Coming of The Wedge

BEFORE Joyce Gibbs could sink into despondency again she saw Doc come out of the cabin and started towards him with Dusty at her side.

"I've fixed his back, ma'am," Doc drawled. "Cleaned the wounds and got them covered. It's bad enough. He'll likely carry the scars until he dies and it'll hurt like hell for a time. But there's no injury to his spine as far as I can tell."

"We can't move him, then?" Dusty asked.

"From where he lies to the bed is all," Doc replied. "Happen you mean can we take him out of here."

"That's what I meant. Rusty, lend a hand to tote him to his bed. Then get your hoss and head back to the herd. Ask Stone if he can send a few of the crew to lend a hand up this ways. Tell him what's happened and that I'll likely come down and see him in the morning, but to get the boys here if he can spare them."

"Yo!" replied Rusty, giving the cavalry affirmative answer.

"Lasalle's place is over that way. Happen you see it, call on in and tell Mark I won't see him until morning."

Joyce watched the men heading into her house. It took some getting used to, the way the two men jumped to obey the small Texan, a man she would have passed in the street without a second glance. Of course she had heard of Dusty Fog, but never would she have pictured him as this small, insignificant cowhand.

Following the two men into the house she watched the gentle way they carried her husband into the bedroom and laid him on the bed, face down. She also blushed at some of the *sotto voce* comments Doc heaped on his friends if they did not

handle Ralph in the manner he felt correct. Already the laudanum had started to wear off and Ralph groaned in pain.

"Just stay by him, ma'am," Doc said. "Until he's sane
enough to know better, I mean wtih the pain and all, and
strong enough to get out of it, we'll have to make sure he
keeps his face from burying into the pillow. I'd stay on, but
I'll see what Dusty wants first."

He left Joyce with her husband and headed out to find
Dusty watching Rusty ride off.

"What now?" Doc asked.

"We'd best put the hosses in the barn first, then get set for a
long wait and maybe a fight."

They took their mounts to the stable and found that the
damage had been done only to the outer walls. So they removed their double girthed saddles and left the horses in
empty stalls, then headed for the house, taking the saddles
with them.

Dusty spent the rest of the afternoon helping Joyce do what
she could about the damage to the house. They set the table up
and found that two chairs remained unbroken, but the rest
were smashed beyond repair. Dusty swore again that he would
make the men behind the raid pay for what they did and he
meant it in more ways than one.

"Your husband's awake, ma'am," Doc said, just before
dark as he entered the room. "Come on in and see him."

Joyce followed the slim Texan into the bedroom and found
her husband, his face lined with pain still, looking at her
although he still lay on his face.

"I'd like to thank you gents for helping us," Ralph Gibbs
said, looking at Dusty who followed his wife into the room.

"There's no call for that," Dusty replied. "I only wish that
I got here in time to stop them doing what they did."

"You fed our guests, honey?" Ralph asked.

"I did the best I could," she answered. "Used some of the
chickens the men killed, made up enough for us all. I'll fetch
you some broth in."

"You fixing on sticking here?" Dusty asked. "If you are,
I'll have some men on hand to help fight off that Double K
bunch when they come."

"I'm staying!" stated Gibbs firmly. "Although how I'll
manage for food I don't know. That bunch told me the only

way we could buy supplies was to sell out to Mallick and he'd give us a note for the store.''

"I've got an answer for that," Dusty said quietly. "How about your market herd, did you get it gathered?"

"Not yet. I wanted to hire a couple of hands for a roundup but there's none to be had out this way."

"We'll see what we can do," promised Dusty. "So—Douse the lights Doc. We've got callers."

They all heard the rapid drumming of hooves and this time not just one horse but several.

Doc quickly doused the light in the room and Dusty darted across to blow out the lamp on the dining-room table. The house plunged into darkness and Dusty stood by a window. He heard a soft footfall and saw Doc coming towards him.

"You ought to be with her," Dusty said.

"That's what I thought," replied Doc and his teeth gleamed white in a grin. "Only I done fetched in, cleaned and loaded that old ten gauge and Mrs. Gibbs done got it by the window, swears to fill the hide of the first Double K skunk she sees out there. She'll do it, too, or I've never seen a gal who could."

"I reckon she will," agreed Dusty for he knew Joyce had regained control of herself and was the more dangerous for it. Now she could handle the shotgun in cold determination and she knew how to make the most of it.

Nearer thundered the hooves. Clearly if these were the Double K they did not expect trouble from Gibbs or his wife. Joyce suddenly realized the riders did not come from the direction of the Double K and she turned from the window to call out this information to Dusty. A voice let out a cowhand yell from the darkness, before she could speak.

"Hey Dusty, Doc! Don't go fanning any lead. It's us."

Which left a lot unexplained to Gibbs and his wife, but apparently satisfied the two men in the dining-room. After a brief pause a match rasped and the table lamp lit once more. Joyce saw Dusty resting his carbine against the wall then open the door they had repaired.

"I can't think of a better reason for shooting!" he called to the men outside, then looked across the room towards Joyce. "It's all right, ma'am. They're friends."

Saying that Dusty stepped out of the house to greet his old friends of the Wedge trail crew.

Six men sat their horses in a half circle before the front of the Gibbs' house. Six men who, apart from the OD Connected crew or some of his illustrious kin, Dusty would rather have seen than any others at such a time. Rusty Willis was one, leaning on his saddlehorn at the right of the party. Next to him, tall, slim, still retaining some of his cavalryman's stiff-backed grace, sat Stone Hart. He would have been a hand-some young man had it not been for the sabre scar on his right cheek, a memento of a cavalry clash in the War Between The States. He wore cowhand clothes neither better nor worse than those of the others, but about him hung the undefinable something which sets a leader of men apart from the others. Stone Hart was such a leader of men. He rode as trail boss for the Wedge and that took a leader, not a driver of men.

"Rusty allows you found some trouble, Dusty," Stone said, his voice an even cultured deep south drawl.

"You called it right, Stone," Dusty agreed, then threw a glance at the woman in the doorway. "Can they light a spell, ma'am?"

"Of course they may," she answered, annoyed at being so lax in her hospitality. "Please get down, gentlemen."

Now she was no longer scared and half-hysterical, Joyce could tell quality when she saw it. Every man in that group looked like a tophand, even the medium sized, stocky man with the drooping moustache and the woe-begone look on his face. The rest did not look like hired hard-cases, but they did look like remarkably efficient fighting men. He alone did not fit into the picture, or the sort to be tied in with such an outfit as the Wedge. Later she found this man, Peaceful Gunn by name, would move easily two inches out of his way if he ran into trouble. His element was a fight into which he could plunge, all the time insisting he was a peace-loving and easy-going as a dove. Joyce knew something of wild animals and knew the dove, for all its being regarded as the bird of peace, was in reality amongst the toughest and most trouble-hunting of birds, always ready for a fight.

Next to Peaceful sat a tall, wide shouldered, freckle faced and handsome young man with a fiery thatch of red hair. He wore cowhand clothes and belted a low handing Army Colt. He rode as scout for the Wedge. Folks said Johnny Raybold, as the red head was named, could eat as much as would founder a good-sized horse although he preferred something more nourishing than grass. he had other good qualities and could be relied on in any man's fight.

While the other three men were not members of Stone Hart's regular crew, all carried a look of tophands who knew what their guns could be used for. They were the usual type of men he hired, tough, salty, loyal to the brand they rode for. Stone introduced them as Tex, Shaun and Billy.

The men trooped into the house at Joyce's invitation. She watched Peaceful as he peered around him a shade nervously. His moustache, which was capable of more expression than most folks could get from their entire face, dropped miserably and gave him the appearance of a terrified walrus.

"Where they at?" he asked in a tone which suggested they might be hiding under the table ready to jump him. "It's getting so a body can't ride a trail these days without running into fuss."

The rest of the men ignored Peaceful's words. Johnny Raybold gave out a whoop and held out a hand to Dusty.

"Where at's thishere wire, Dusty?" he asked. "And where's Mark 'n' the Kid?"

"What you want them for?" groaned Peaceful, his moustache drooping like the wilted lily on a cheap undertaker's lapel. "They'll only help wind us up in more trouble."

This brought howls of derision from the others who all knew Peaceful much better than did Joyce.

"Should head for the badlands and go 'round," he went on miserably. "That way we won't wind up in fuss with them gents who strung the wire."

"Get mum, all of you," Stone growled, bringing an end to the argument which was developing, even before it started. "We all know you'd be fit to be tied if I even thought of going round."

"Rusty tell you it all, Stone?" Dusty asked, while Joyce went to fetch coffee for her guests.

"What he knew about it. What's on that tricky Rio Hondo mind?"

"I figured that Double K might come back and that'd we'd give 'em a real Texas welcome, only I needed a few friends on hand to tote 'round the tea and biscuits for the guests."

Stone Hart smiled. He'd known Dusty for a few years now

and they'd sided each other in a couple of tight spots in that time. One thing he did know for sure. The situation up here must be very grave for Dusty to send for help during a drive. Dusty knew trail driving, knew it from the angle of hand and as trail boss, so he would not lightly send and ask for men.

"Stake 'em out the way you want," he said, setting the seal of approval on Dusty's actions and giving permission for orders to be passed to his men. Stone hired the men, it should be to him to make any arrangements for their employment, but he knew Dusty had a better idea of the situation and knew what would be needed in offence and defence.

"I'll have Johnny staked out on the range about a mile out towards the Double K, waiting for the first sound of their coming. When they get here I want some of the boys in the out-buildings, some here. I want that bunch boxed in and held tighter than a Yankee storekeeper's purse strings."

"Get to it, Johnny," drawled Stone. "Which's the way Double K'll most likely come ma'am?"

"That way," Joyce answered, a finger stabbing in the direction of the Double K house. "But they might not come that direction."

"It's likely they will," Dusty replied. "They don't know about Stone and the boys and'll likely think they've got nothing to worry about. So they'll come the easiest direction."

"Dusty could be right at that, ma'am," Stone put in.

Joyce noticed the trail boss never looked straight at her and tried to keep the unscarred side of his face to her all the time. She felt sorry for him, he must have been a really handsome young man before the Yankee sabre marred his face. Even now a woman would not find him revolting; the scar looked bad, but could have been far worse. Much as she wished to tell him her thoughts she knew any reference to his injury would offend Stone. He would not want a stranger to mention it.

The men stood around Joyce's table and drank their coffee, all except Johnny who knew what was expected of him and faded off into the dark astride his big iron grey night horse. Only Peaceful seemed to be worried by the forthcoming possible visit and Joyce got the feeling that he did not care as much as he pretended.

"What do you want from the rest of us, Dusty?" asked Rusty Willis.

"Stone, Doc and I'll stay at the house," Dusty answered with a grin. "And don't go saying we're pulling rank on you—because we are. Rest of you pick out your places and wait until you hear Johnny come back. Put your hosses in the barn, but keep them saddled. If Double K hit, I want them. Not one's got to get back to their spread."

"These Double K bunch, Cap'n Fog," put in one of the new Wedge hands, "How'd you want them, alive or dead?"

"Whichever way you have to take them."

Dusty's reply came in a flat, even voice, but every man present knew what he meant. Shoot if you must and if you must shoot, shoot to kill, that was Dusty's meaning. It was the way of a tough lawman, of the man who tamed Quiet Town. Such would be the orders he gave to his deputies when they went after a dangerous outlaw in the line of duty. In the same manner Dusty now spoke. He did not want killings or trouble, but if Double K forced them on him he would try and prevent his side from taking lead if he could.

"How about me, Dusty?" asked Joyce after the men went to their posts. She used his given name, having received no encouragement to carry on with his formal rank and title, and knowing far better than call a cowhand "mister" after being introduced.

"If they come, get in the bedroom with your man. Let Doc handle the fighting, he'll be in there. Stone, Johnny and I'll be out here."

"Don't you think it might be better to send that miserable looking man back to the herd?" she asked. "He looked terrified when he went out to the barn."

Two faces looked at her, trying to see if she was joking, then Dusty and Stone started grinning.

"You mean Peaceful, ma'am?" asked Stone.

"I don't know his name. Nobody got around to introducing me to any of you."

Taking the hint Dusty introduced her to Stone. She knew the Wedge boss by reputation but nothing more. He and Dusty seemed much alike in many ways. Polite, courteous, yet masterful. Men who gave orders and knew their strength without being over-aggressive or bullying. She could see how they extracted such loyalty from the men under their command.

"How many men do you have, Stone?" Dusty asked, forgetting the matter of sending Peaceful to the safety of the herd.

"My regular crew and nine more."

"Seventeen, huh? Double K have at least that many at the spread and more in town. You'll be needing half of your men to hold the herd back down there for a day or two while we sort this wire trouble out."

"There's folks relying on me taking their herds through, Dusty," Stone pointed out.

"I've thought about that too."

"What're you fixing to do then?"

"Wait hereabouts for Clay Allison to come closer, ride down tomorrow and meet him, ask for help."

Stone grunted. "I never knowed the Wedge to need Clay Allison to do our fighting for us."

"He's not fighting for you. He's fighting for himself, for every herd that comes up the trail, for every man who died making this trail and keeping it open in the early days," Dusty answered. "And I hope to keep it from busting into an open fight if I can."

"It'll come to fighting, happen Clay reaches here and the wire's still up," Stone answered.

"Not the way I want to play it. With him and your boys I reckon we have enough hard-country stock to make Double K think twice about locking horns."

"Would Clay Allison make all that much difference?" Joyce asked, looking from one man to the other.

"Enough, ma'am," Stone answered.

He knew Clay Allison, respected the man as a rancher and a trail boss of the first water, but there had never been any close ties between them. To Stone the end of a trail meant little more than selling his herd at the best possible price, paying off his hands, working out each ranch's share of the profits and taking his cut to be added to the bank balance with which he hoped one day soon to buy a ranch of his own.

To Clay Allison, already a rich rancher owner in his own right, the end of a drive meant fun, hoorawing the trail-end town, celebrations, wild and hectic parties with his hands and anyone who cared to join in the fun, before heading back home to Texas. Happen there should also be a chance to tie into some loud-mouth Kansas lawman who boasted he jailed Texans one handed, left-handed at that, then Clay Allison's trail-end was made complete.

So, beyond their mutual loyalty to the south in the War and their combined interest in keeping open a trail to the Kansas markets, Clay Allison and Stone Hart had little or nothing in common. Yet Stone knew Clay's name packed considerable weight as a fast-gun fighting man. With him along, backed by the Wedge's men, Dusty might be able to make the owner of the Double K open the trail without blood being shed.

"I'd like to leave three men here and send three across to the Jones spread, if that rides all right with you, Stone," Dusty drawled. "Just for a couple of days happen all goes well."

"Sure, I'll see to it," Stone replied. "We've made good time up to here and the beef could stand a couple of days' rest. I'll leave Rusty, Doc and Billy here."

Hearing the words Joyce could almost have sung with delight. She knew Rusty looked like he could take care of himself and any of the other hands, apart from the one called Peaceful, would also be a good man to have around. She decided Doc was being left to help care for her husband, although he did wear a fast man's gun-rig, she doubted if so studious a looking young man could make best use of it.

"Which spread's the further from Double K?" Dusty asked. "You or Jones?"

"We are."

"Be best to have Peaceful up there then. Should be far enough away from Double K to keep him happy," Dusty said.

"But we're farther from Double K—!" Joyce began, thinking Dusty misunderstood her words.

"Yes'm, that's just what we mean," grinned Stone.

Leaving Joyce to try and work logic out of the words, Dusty and Stone got down to discussing the events leading up to this night gathering. Joyce sighed, deciding she would never understand cowhands. She went into the bedroom to find her husband sleeping comfortably and Doc sitting by the window, cleaning his Army Colt.

Sitting his horse about a mile from the ranch house Johnny Raybold looked around him, studying the open range. Then he swung down and squat on his heels, letting his iron grey stallion stand with reins dangling. Tied or loose the big horse would not stray far from him, and never played up or tried to avoid him when he went to it. That was a quality Johnny often needed in his task as scout for the Wedge.

Johnny drew his Winchester from the saddleboot and then settled down for a long wait. He took out his makings, rolling a smoke and hanging it from the corner of his mouth, but did not offer to light it. The horse moved to one side and fell to cropping the grass.

"Fool chore this, ole hoss," he said quietly, after being on watch for an hour. "Bet Chow put Dusty up to it."

Snorting softly the horse moved closer to its master. Johnny grinned, realizing that Dusty could not have seen the Wedge's cook for a couple of years and could hardly have worked up this business with chow. It made him feel better to lay the blame on somebody for being sent on a chore that he, with the exception of the Ysabel Kid, could handle best.

Johnny knew little or nothing of the trouble in this section of the Panhandle country. He had been with the rest of the crew when Rusty Willis returned on the run with a message for Stone. Johnny found himself one of the group Stone selected to ride with him, leaving his segundo, Waggles Harrison, in charge of the herd. Why they came still remained something of a mystery to Johnny. He did not particularly care. A good friend needed help and Johnny needed to know no more.

Listening to the night noises Johnny stayed where he was, quiet, relaxed and without moving restlessly. Often he had done this kind of work and knew how to keep his mind alert and working without it interfering with his watching and listening. He thought of nights spent sitting by a fire, listening to the baying of coon-hound music as a redbone ran a line in the darkness. To Johnny no sound in the world came so sweetly as the trail song of a good hound dog. He thought of his return to Texas for the fall. He'd head down and see some kin who owned good hounds and—

Suddenly the thoughts ended. Johnny came to his feet in a lithe move. He stood with the rifle held before his body, face turned towards the sound which took his thoughts from hound music. For a moment he stood, listening to the night sounds and catching once more the faint crackle of shots in the distance.

Now Johnny had a problem on his hands. He did not know

if Dusty could hear the shots while in the house. So Johnny needed to decide if to stay here or head back with the word would be best. Then he decided. Dusty would want to know about the shooting, especially as there did not appear to be any sign of the Double K.

Johnny turned, he went afork his stallion in a bound, catching up the reins and starting his mount running towards the house.

In the house Joyce poured her coffee for her guests before making for the barn and serving the other men. She stifled a yawn and said, "They might not be coming tonight after all."

"Might not," agreed Dusty. "But—"

They all heard the thunder of a fast running horse's hooves and made for the door of the house. Outside they could just hear the crackle of shots. Joyce's face lost some of its colour.

"Lasalle's!" she gasped.

By now the other men were from the barn. A sudden bright flash showed down where the shots sounded, followed by a dull booming roar.

"Dynamite!" Dusty snapped. "Loan me a hoss, Stone. I've got to get down there."

Stone wasted no time. "Peaceful, loan Dusty your hoss. Stay here with Doc. The rest of you hit those kaks and let's ride."

For a man who professed to have no other aim in life but to avoid trouble, Peaceful showed some reluctance to being left out of the rescue party. He did not argue for he knew Mark Counter was out there some place, most likely where that explosion sounded. He led his big horse from the barn and jerked the Spencer rifle from the saddleboot.

Dusty went astride Peaceful's horse in a flying mount, grabbed the reins and put his pet-makers to work. The horse was no livery plug to accept a stranger on its back, but it sensed a master rider and did not try to make a fight. It set off across the darkened range at a gallop. The other men followed. They rode fast, pushing their horses. For all they knew, their help might be needed at Lasalle's place.

In the lead Dusty rode with fear in his heart. The dynamite had gone off at the Lasalle place and his *amigo*, a man as close as any brother, might even now be dead, blown to doll-rags by the Double K hired killers.

CHAPTER ELEVEN

The Hit At LaSalle's

"I'LL see that five thousand dollars and up another five," Freda Lasalle announced calmly, after studying the three kings in her hand once more.

The Lasalle's sitting-room looked bright and cheerful enough. Lasalle sat at the side table, reading a book and throwing his amused gaze at the high stake poked game at the dining table where his daughter backed feminine intuition against the skill and knowledge of the other two. Female intuition did not seem to be all it was cracked up to be for Freda owed Mark and Morg Summers about five hundred thousand dollars so far.

"I sure can't see how you always get the cards," she objected, after the betting as her three kings fell before Mark's low straight.

"Unlucky in love, lucky at cards," Mark answered.

An over-done snigger greeted his words, coming from Freda who reached for the cards. The game only started to stop her worrying about the fate of her friends and the non-arrival of Dusty, Rusty and Doc. On his ride to the herd Rusty had missed Lasalle's place and so none of the occupants knew what might have kept Dusty away. At last Mark insisted they played cards, needling Freda into the game to prevent her worrying.

To Morg Summers the night could go on for ever. He now held the position as official hand of the Lasalle spread and Freda seemed very friendly. Morg wondered how things stood between the girl and Mark Counter, felt just a little jealous and decided he did not have a chance against such a handsome

and famous man's opposition. However he got the idea that
Mark would be riding out as soon as the trouble came to an
end and felt better about things.

The redbone hound sprawled before the empty fireplace for
Mark would not allow a fire. Suddenly the dog raised his
head, looking towards the front door and letting a low growl
rumble deep in his throat.

"Douse the lights!" Mark snapped, thrusting back his
chair. "Get to your places. Move it!"

His very urgency put life into their limbs. Morg blew out the
lamp on the table and Lasalle doused the other. They could all
hear the horses now, a fair sized bunch of them by all accounts. It looked like Tring had returned and meant to make
up for his last visit and so brought plenty of help.

"Hit the back, Morg!" Mark ordered. "George, take that
side and watch the barn. Freda, keep well down, gal. Don't
none of you start throwing lead until I give the word."

For once Freda did not make any comment to Mark's
orders. She knew when to have a joke and when to obey fast,
without question. Mark had been in charge of the prepara-
tions for defending the house ever since they returned from
town. He threw all his considerable knowledge into the
matter. First he scouted around and found a secluded draw
about two miles from them and on the side away from Double
K. Into this went all the ranch's remuda along with Dusty and
Mark's horses and their pack horse. Then, although he ached
in every muscle and bone, Mark looked the house over and
found but little needed attending to, beyond dousing the
dining-room fire and making sure all the weapons were fully
loaded.

Now the attack had come. The riders were on top of the
slope and coming down towards the river. Suddenly shots
thundered out, lead smashed into the house but its walls kept
them out. The window panes shattered and bullets raked the
room, but so far all the shooting came from the front.

Mark's matched guns were in his hands as he flattened on
the wall by the window. He looked back across the room, eyes
trying to pierce the darkness. From the look of things the
opening volley hit nobody. He could see Lasalle's shape by the
side window looking out towards the barn and outbuildings,
holding his Le Mat carbine ready for use. Morg had already

taken his place in the hands' bedroom and so would be clear. That only left Freda.

"Mark!" whispered a scared voice at his side, a voice trying to hide its fear. "I've brought your rifle. Papa and Morg are in place and ready. Why did those men start shooting?"

Before Mark could make a reply the Double K men came sweeping down the slope and into the water. He guessed that whoever had charge of the raid thought the occupants of the houses were all asleep and hoped to startle and confuse himself and his friends. The men knew of the hound's presence and that a chance of moving in silently was unlikely to succeed. So they hoped to startle, suddenly waken the people in the house and rush in on them before they recovered.

It was a real smart plan. Except that Mark and the others were fully awake and ready.

Suddenly Mark swung around towards the shattered window. He brought up his right-hand Colt, thumbing four rapid shots into the darkness, firing into the brown without taking sight. He heard a yell and guessed some of the lead took effect. The attackers yelled their surprise. He heard the frantic churning of hooves in water as they brought their horses to a halt or tried to change directions. Mark grinned and darted to the other window, beyond the door.

"Pour it into them, Dusty!" he yelled, firing three more shots, and trying to make out his two *amigos* were with him.

He heard the crash of his rifle from the window just vacated and twisted his head in time to see Freda flatten herself back against the wall. The girl once more showed she had courage and could think for herself. She guessed at what he tried to do and lent a hand.

The riders came ashore and fanned out, riding along the side of the house towards the barn. Lasalle cut loose with the old Le Mat, turning four of his nine bullets adrift towards the men. He did not think he had managed to hit anyone but his little effort caused a rapid swing about and dart to cover.

Not all the men had headed for the barn, a few went the other way but Mark already had thought of this and was by the other side window which stood open. He lined his right-hand Colt and used its last two loads on them. This time he saw a man crumple over, cling to his saddlehorn and turn his horse away.

"Freda!" Mark snapped. "Watch 'em, gal. I'll reload."

It took some time to strip foil from a combustile cartridge, nick the bottom to ensure the percussion cap's spark of flame struck powder, and place it in the chamber of the Colt, turn the chamber, work the loading rammer and force it home. Mark had done the drill so often he could manage it in daylight or dark, but he felt satisfied with himself that he remembered to have the spare loads laid out on the table, along with an open percussion cap box. He loaded both his guns and even as he did so fresh developments came.

The men from Double K, being met with a hot fire on three sides of the house, took stock of the situation. From the guns, and the yell they heard, it looked like Dusty Fog, Mark Counter and Lasalle were all in front and, unless Dune called it wrong, the Ysabel Kid had left for Bent's Ford. So it appeared the defenders had committed an error in tactics and left the rear unguarded. With this in mind a group of men moved in, swinging behind the barn, leaving their horses and running off across the range, meaning to come in at the rear.

"Hey, Freda!" Morg's voice came in an urgent whisper. "Bring me some shells for my rifle, please."

"I'll be right there," she answered.

"It's no use you-all trying to make me jealous, gal," drawled Mark. "I'm allus true to one gal—at a time."

"She doesn't show very good taste, whoever she is," replied Freda hotly, but in no louder voice than Mark used. "I wouldn't be your gal, Mark Counter, not even if you were the last man in the world."

"Gal," replied Mark, his teeth gleaming in a grin as he watched her back off from the table, keeping down. "Was I the last man in the world I'd be too busy to worry."

Freda gave a snort and thought of a suitable answer, although she doubted if her father would approve of it. She collected a box of bullets and headed for the bedroom to find Morg standing by an open window and looking out. He had his rifle in his hands, but her ten gauge lay on the bed by his side.

"Hi, there," he greeted. "Sure is quiet back here. Say, has that mean ole Mark been abusing you again?"

"He sure has. Whyn't you act like a knight in shining armour and go in there to demand satisfaction."

"Me?" grinned Morg. "I'm satisfied already. Who wouldn't be? Got me a starlit night, a real pretty gal to talk to and—hand me up the scatter, gal."

None of the speech had been in a loud tone, but the last few words came in an urgent whisper. Freda took up the shotgun, exchanging it for the rifle he offered her. Then she peered through the window and watched the dark shapes moving by the backhouse and coming towards them.

Gripping the shotgun Morg rested its barrels on the window ledge and drew back the hammers. The double click must have sounded loud in the still of the night, the group of men out back came to a halt for a moment. Then, apparently deciding the clicks to be imagination they moved forward, their weapons glinting dully in their hands.

Morg now had a problem. Never had he been in such a spot and he had never turned lead loose at another man. He did not want to shoot at the men, to kill without a warning. Then an idea came to him.

"She's loaded with nine buckshot, gents!" he called. "Hereby I lets her go! Yahoo! Hunt your holes, you gophers!"

His first words brought the men to an uneasy halt. The rest of his speech had the effect of making the men turn about and head for cover. He aimed low and cut loose with both barrels. A man yelled, staggered, but reeled on. Morg knew some of the lead had gone home but that the man he hit was not seriously hurt.

He passed the shotgun to Freda who whispered she would reload for him. At the shot, lead slashed from all sides at the house. A bullet smashed into the window frame, showering broken glass and splinters which caused Freda to cry out and twist around. Morg gave an angry growl, grabbing his rifle to throw shots at the spurts of flame around the building.

"Are you all right?" he asked.

The concern in his voice brought a thrill to Freda, a thrill she could hardly explain even to herself. Before she could answer the firing died down and Mark's voice came to her.

"How's it going back there? Is the roof still on?"

"Why shouldn't it be?" Freda replied, running a hand across her face and knowing the flying splinters missed her.

"I heard you fire that fool shotgun off!"

It took Freda a moment to catch Mark's meaning. She wished she could find a real smart answer. Then she remembered Morg's question and turned to him, seeing he watched her.

"I'm all right thanks, Morg. How about you?"

She laid a hand on his arm, he released the rifle with one hand to reach and trap the hand, holding it gently.

"Lord!" he said. "If they'd hurt you I'd—"

Freda bent forward, her lips lightly brushed his cheek. This was not the action of a well brought-up young lady. She and Morg met for the first time that afternoon, sure he had taken on to ride for her father but that did not mean he took on for any other reason than he needed work. All those thoughts buzzed through Freda's head after her impulsive action.

"There's nothing between Mark and me," she whispered.

"There's no gal any place waiting for me," Morg whispered.

Then they kissed, oblivious of everything. Two young people who suddenly found themselves in love. Then Morg gently moved her away from him and swung to the window. Any man who tried to harm Freda was going to get lead and would need to kill him first.

Unaware of romance blooming in the back of the house Mark Counter moved from front to the left side of the dining-room, watching through the windows, letting the Double K men do the shooting, saving his lead for when it would be needed to break an attack.

He flattened by the side of the window which looked out across the range. Men darted forward, coming towards the house. Then a shout from the other side reached his ears although he could not make out the words. The approaching party came to a halt and took cover rapidly.

Mark's fighting instincts warned him something was in the air. The men had been moving in undetected, or at least without warning that they had been detected. Yet they had taken cover in a hurry. This was not the actions he would expect of an attacking group coming in to their objective unsuspected. Anything unusual in an attack worried Mark and made him the more alert.

"Freda!" he called. "Freda!"

The second word brought her to his side. She realized that he no longer sounded easy-going and friendly.

"Go and warn both your pappy and Morg to be ready for something to start. That bunch out there have something tricky on their minds."

"What?" she asked.

"I wish I knew, gal."

The coldness of his voice made her feel as if a chilly hand laid itself on her. She knew Mark had guessed what the smart move might be—and that it was something terrible.

After delivering Mark's message to her father Freda returned to the bedroom and told Morg. He gripped her hand in his.

"Are you scared?" he asked.

"Not now I'm with you."

At the right side window Lasalle knelt watching the barn into which a fair part of the attacking force went. Due to Mark's prompt action on returning from Barlock they would find little to destroy and would not burn the building until after the attack. A lighted barn blazing merrily would make them much too easy targets for the defenders, so the barn and other buildings were safe during the attack.

Nursing the Le Mat, feeling the weight of the Army Colt in his waistband, he watched for the first sign of his attackers. He wished he could take time out to reload the fired chambers, but still had a fair few shots left and a load of grapeshot in the lower barrel, just waiting to be used.

Lasalle was no longer the defeated, tired man who rode to his ranch that morning, ready to call "calf-rope" and run. Now he stood firm, grimly determined to fight for his home, to defend it with his last breath.

A small group of men eased out of the barn, moving cautiously towards the house. Lasalle watched them, wondering if his best move would be to open fire now, or let them come in closer and make sure he hit at least one of them. He did not want to kill, but knew it might be necessary to get himself clear of this mess. He knew they did not suspect he watched them, or they would not be advancing so openly on him.

Just as he decided to throw a warning shot, the group halted. He saw a flicker of light, a glow as if a man had turned around and lit a match, shielding the flame with his body. Apparently one of the men had lit a cigarette or cigar, for something glowed redly in the darkness.

In a flash Lasalle knew something to be dead wrong. He knew that in the heat and madness of battle men often did strange things like singing, praying, crying or shouting. But they did not stop to light cigarettes. Nor did men sneaking up on a night attack a defended building.

Resting the barrel of the carbine on the window he took a careful aim. Drawing back the hammer he fired a shot and saw the man holding the red, glowing thing rock under the impact of lead, then go down, dropping whatever he held so that it spluttered on the ground by him.

Instantly consternation and pandemonium reigned amongst the party around the shot man. They yelled, shouted, and one bent, grabbing at the spluttering red glow on the ground. The others seemed to panic and not one of them thought to throw lead at the house. Lasalle aimed again, switching to the grapeshot barrel and touching off a shot, sending it into the body of the man bending to grab the thing from the ground.

Then the others turned, racing away, not merely running, but fleeing in terror, discarding their rifles as they went. They left a man sprawled on his back and another crawling on hands and knees, screaming after them.

"Dave! Stace!" he screamed in a voice none of the others who heard it would forget. "Come back he—!"

The rest ended in a thunderous roar and a sheet of flame which ripped the night apart, turning it for a brief instant, into day. The house shook, the remaining window glass shattered in the explosion's blast, but the walls held firm.

"Get to the windows!" Mark roared. "Pour it into them!"

His words came not a moment too soon. Hooves thundered, feet thudded and men shouted as they raced towards the house. Freda dashed into the front room with Morg's rifle in her hands. She reached the window and fired through it at the horsemen rushing up from the river. She heard the rapid crashing of Mark's rifle, saw a man drop from his horse and fired again. From the bedroom sounded the booming roar of the shotgun. Her father's Le Mat spat at the side and lead raked and ripped into the house.

"Mark!" Freda screamed, seeing a shape loom up at the window on the undefended side.

Mark turned, levering two shots, the first struck the wall close to the window, the second slammed into the man's face and threw him back from it.

A man sprang from his horse, landed before Freda's window and grabbed the rifle in her hands. She screamed, her finger closed on the trigger and flame lashed from the barrel. She saw the man reel back, smelled burning cloth and flesh, then screamed and fell to the floor in a faint.

His rifle empty, Mark let it fall to the floor and brought out the matched Colt guns. Now he was at his most deadly for he could handle the Colts like twin extensions of his own arms. Flame spurted from the left gun, causing a rapid withdrawal from the side window just as a man tried to throw down on him. A sound before the house brought him around, throwing a bullet into the shoulder of a mounted rider and causing him to turn his horse and head away.

Lasalle cut loose with his Le Mat, shooting fast and emptying the cylinder. Then he let the gun drop and drew the Army Colt to shoot again. He stopped one man with the Colt, which surprised him as he had never been much of a hand with a revolver.

At the back Morg's shotgun brought a hurried end to the attack and left one man moaning on the ground. The young cowhand felt sick, but the heat of the excitement kept it down. He had put lead into a man, maybe killed him. It was not a pleasant thought.

Then it was over. The defence had been too hot and accurate for hired guns to face. They broke off, dragging their dead and wounded with them, making for their horses. They split into two parties, one throwing lead at the house while the other mounted dead and wounded on horseback for they wished to leave as little proof as possible. Those were Mallick's orders when he organized the attack by almost the full Double K crew with the intention of wiping Lasalle's place from the face of the earth. Dusty Fog and Mark Counter had good friends who would come and investigate should they be killed. Nothing which might point to Double K must be found. The same applied now. Sure the men in the house knew who was responsible for the attack—but they couldn't prove it and Elben was the only law around.

"You can light the lamps now," Mark said as the men rode away, splashing through the water. "The mauling we gave them—My God! Freda!"

Almost before he reached her side Morg had arrived and Lasalle ran to where the girl lay on the floor.

She groaned and Mark struck a match, looking for some sign of a wound. He saw the fear and panic in her eyes. She stared wildly at him.

"What—where—!"

"Easy gal. They've gone," Mark replied. "Are you hit?"

"I killed one of them!" she gasped. "I shot—"

"Drop it, girl!" Mark's voice cracked like a whip. "It was him or you. Now lie easy until we find if he hit you."

Morg lit the lamp and stared at the girl in a distracted manner. Not until then did he feel the trickle of blood running down his face where one of the last shots threw splinters into him. Freda saw it and nothing could have shaken her out of the hysteria quicker.

"Morg!" she gasped, getting to her feet. "You're hurt!"

"Not him," Mark put in. "You can't hurt a feller from Montana by hitting him on the head."

The girl threw Mark a cold look and eased Morg into a chair. She saw the wound to be more messy than dangerous and prepared to care for it. Lasalle watched all this and a slightly puzzled look came to his face. Mark grinned and suggested they took a look outside.

Freda froze as she reached a hand to Morg's head. "That explosion!" she gasped. "What caused it?"

"Dynamite," Mark answered flatly. "Come on, George. Let's make sure they've left clean. Where's that old Bugle dog?"

Having shown commendable good sense and headed for the girl's bedroom when the shooting started, Bugle now came out, wagging his tail. He followed the two men to the door of the house. He stood outside and his head swung to one side, his back hair rose and he growled.

"Back in, *pronto*!" Mark snapped. "Freda, douse the lights."

Once more the room plunged into darkness and Bugle

headed for the safety of his mistress's bedroom.

"Get the guns loaded!" Mark growled. "We might need them."

The horses came nearer and Lasalle's house lay silent. Mark felt puzzled at the turn of events. He thought that after the mauling they took Double K would stay well clear. They might be sending a small group of determined men in, hoping the house suspected nothing, although Mark could not think how the group managed to get in the direction from which they came so soon after departing the other way.

"Yeeah!"

Loud in the night it rang. The old battle yell of the Confederate Cavalry. Mark realized that Dusty would send one of his friends to the Wedge to collect help and reinforcements. The explosion must have brought them on the run but they knew better than ride up unannounced to a house which had just been under attack.

"Hey Mark!" yelled Dusty's voice. "Answer up, *amigo*!"

"Come ahead and quit that fool yelling!" Mark called back. "What for you all waking folks up in the middle of the night?" He holstered his guns and threw a look across the room to where Freda and Morg were much closer than needed for first-aid or reloading weapons. "You can put the lamp on again. Unless you'd rather stay in the dark."

Freda and Morg gave startled and guilty exclamations, moving apart hurriedly and trying to look unconcerned as Lasalle lit the lamp.

"You're so sharp you'll cut yourself, Mark Counter," Freda gasped. "Why don't you go out and meet Dusty?"

"Why sure," agreed Mark. "Reckon you pair would like to be alone."

The nearest thing Freda could lay hands on that wouldn't be too dangerous was the discarded deck of cards. She grabbed them up and hurled them at Mark. He side stepped, grinned, winked at the blushing Morg, then stepped out to greet his friends.

CHAPTER TWELVE

The Map

"You all right, *amigo*?" Dusty asked, swinging down from the borrowed horse and walking towards Mark.

"Why sure. They didn't get any of us."

"What happened?" asked Johnny Raybold, showing his relief at finding Mark safe and unharmed.

"They hit us foot, hoss and artillery," Mark replied, hearing the others as they came from the house behind him.

"Get any of 'em, Mark?" Rusty Willis inquired.

"Not less'n these folks can shoot," scoffed Johnny. "He couldn't hit the side of a barn if he was in it."

Mark ignored the comments from his good friends. He stepped forward to greet Stone Hart and then introduced him to Lasalle, Freda and Morg. They were all invited in, but Johnny and Rusty turned their horses and headed across the stream to make a sweep across the range and make certain the Double K pack had headed home.

"I reckon there were getting on for twenty or more of them," Mark said, as the men gathered around the Lasalle's dining-room table and Freda, with Morg's help, went to the kitchen to make coffee. "They came down on us loaded for bear."

"That's a mean bear, needing dynamite to move it," Dusty answered quietly.

"That's the part of it I don't like," growled Stone. "Dusty, they've gone too far now. We'll have to paint for war."

"Likely. Comes daylight Mark and I'll head down trail and get Clay to come up here. Then we'll clear this whole section out. It'll be open season on anybody wearing a gun and riding for Double K."

Lasalle looked at the faces around the table. Tanned faces which showed little of their thoughts. Not one of them looked like the sort of man to back down once they set their mind to a thing.

"Why did they hit us tonight?" he asked.

"Way I see it, they had to make a grandstand play. They'd hit Gibbs and left him with his hide peeled by a blacksnake whip," Dusty answered. "Which same Pop Jones had called it quits. That left you. If you stayed on the other two might take heart and stand fast. You had to be brought down."

"But not with dynamite, Dusty," Stone Hart objected. "That's going a mite strong even for a bunch of hard-cases with the local law behind them."

"Maybe," Dusty drawled. "I'll feel happier when I've got Clay Allison here so we can make us some talk to the owner of the Double K."

"Something struck me about this Keller," Lasalle put in. "None of the Double K crowd even refer to him. When they say boss they always mean Mallick."

"Maybe haven't seen enough of Keller to call him boss," Mark answered.

"Or maybe he's not the real boss of this she-bang," Stone suggested. "It could be that Mallick's behind all this for his own benefit. Nobody's seen Keller from all accounts."

They were words of wisdom, although none of the others knew it. However before the subject could be followed further Rusty Willis returned with word that Johnny had taken off after the Double K men and would not be back for a couple of hours. Rusty had taken time out to circle the house on his return.

"Looks like you got at least four, maybe more," he said, then looked at Lasalle. "Was I you, I'd keep my gal inside comes morning."

"Why?"

"It's not a sight for her to see. Out where the dynamite went off," was the simple reply. "I'd say at least two of them were there, but it's kinda hard to tell for sure."

"Two's right," Lasalle said, his voice showing strain and a shudder running through his body. "One of them was wounded. I hit—"

"Drop it!" Mark snapped, gripping the man's shoulder in a

hold which made him wince and brought an end to his words. "You didn't ask them to come here in the night, or to try and dynamite your home. And it damned sure wasn't your fault they came to die."

"Mark's right at that, friend," agreed Stone Hart. "You stopped a man killing you, your daughter, Mark and that young feller in the kitchen. To do that you shot a man who was trying to throw dynamite at your place. It was his choosing, not you'rn."

Dusty thrust back his chair and came to his feet. He went to the kitchen door, opened it, closed it again, without Morg and Freda knowing for they were in each other's arms and kissing. Dusty knocked on the door, turning to wink at the others. Then he opened it and walked in. Now Freda busied herself at the stove and Morg seemed fully occupied with cutting bread for her.

"We'll be staying here for the night, Freda," he said. "Stone and the boys don't have their bedrolls along."

"I'll fix it," she replied, face just a trifle flushed.

An hour later Freda went to her room and climbed into bed. She heard the men settling down in the dining-room and wondered if she would sleep again, so great was the feeling surging inside her as she thought of Morg Summers. She doubted if sleep would ever come to her again.

Yells and whoops woke Freda. For a moment she lay on her bed, blinking in daylight which flooded her room. Then she gasped for she saw the sun hung higher in the sky than usually was the case when she rose. Rolling from her bed she sat on the edge, rubbing her eyes. Then she went to the window and peered out. She stared at the sight before her, wondering what had gone wrong for it seemed that Johnny Raybold and Rusty Willis were attacking Dusty Fog.

Freda had undressed and wore her night-gown now; she could not remember doing it the previous night, but appeared to have done so. Grabbing up her robe she quickly climbed into it. She saw Rusty grab Dusty from behind, locking hands around his waist from behind. Johnny had landed on the ground, but was getting up and charging into the attack.

The girl could not think what started the fight. She wondered why none of the others stopped it. With bare feet slapping on the floor, Freda darted from her room and through the kitchen. She tore open the door and went out. To her amazement her father and the other men sat around watching the fight and clearly enjoying it.

Even as the girl appeared Dusty bent forward, reached between his legs to grab one of Rusty's. Then he straightened and Rusty let out a yell and fell backwards with Dusty sitting down hard on him.

"Eeyow whooof!" Rusty bellowed, the air rammed from his lungs in the cry.

By this time Johnny was on his feet and charging forward. Dusty left the recumbent Rusty's body in a rolling dive forward. His hand clamped on Johnny's ankle in passing and heaved. Johnny gave a wail and lost his balance. He lit down on his hands, breaking his fall with the skill of a horseman taking a toss from a bad one.

Dusty retained his grip on the ankle and grabbed Johnny's free leg. He bent the legs upwards, crossing the ankles and sitting on them. Johnny's mouth opened and he let out a howl.

"Yowee!" he yelled. "Yipes, uncle, Dusty. Uncle!"

Never had Freda felt so completely baffled by a turn of events. She stared at her father, then at Mark and Stone who calmly smoked cigarettes, finally at Morg who seemed to be enjoying the scene.

"What happened?" she gasped, watching Dusty rise after receiving Johnny's surrender howl. "What happened?"

"That?" grinned Mark as the men got to their feet. "Why that's just Johnny 'n' Rusty showing Dusty how it's done."

"But—but—I thought—!" began a very irate Freda. *"Cowhands!"*

With that final yell, realizing that no young lady should be seen dressed, or rather undressed, in such a manner, she turned and fled to the house.

Johnny grinned wryly as he took up his hat. Ever since Dusty demonstrated the arts of ju jitsu and karate to them in Quiet Town, Rusty and he had tried to disprove its effectiveness. Whenever their paths crossed with Dusty's, the two Wedge hands banded together to show their friend they could lick him—only they never managed to do it.

"Say, Dusty," Johnny drawled. "You dropped this paper. Is it anything important?"

He held out a scrap of paper and Dusty frowned. Then the light dawned and Dusty thrust a hand into his levis pocket. He drew out the torn papers taken from Mallick's office on the previous day.

"It might be at that," he said. "Let's go inside and see if we can sort it out."

"I'll get the boys out to those two spreads first," Stone replied. "Then I'd best go down trail to the herd."

Dusty left Stone to attend to the matter and entered the house. He went to the table and sat down, spreading the pieces of paper out before him. Turning them so they all faced the same side upwards he started to fit them together. He found little difficulty in getting the scraps in order and forming a completed whole. A map lay before him, complete in design and outline, but without a single name to say what it might be a map of. It showed land contours, water-courses, woods even, yet not a single letter to identify the range it covered. An oblong outline ran around the inner edge of the map but it meant nothing to him.

"Where in hell is it a map of?" he said, more to himself than to Lasalle who stood by the window.

"Let me take a look, Captain."

For a long moment Lasalle studied the map, frowning and cocking his head on one side.

"I forgot about the pieces," Dusty drawled. "Picked them up in Mallick's office yesterday, but things happened a mite fast and I didn't get a chance to look at them earlier."

Then Dusty tensed slightly. He took a long look at the map, then reached into his pants pocket. He shook his head, rose and crossed the room to where a box of Winchester bullets lay. Taking one out he returned to the table and bent over the map. He drew a line from the lower edge about six inch from the right side to about an inch from the top, then still using the bullet's lead as a pencil, made a right angle turn and a line to the right edge.

"Does it look any more familiar now?" he asked.

Lasalle looked down at the map, he gave an explosive grunt of surprise as he saw the whole thing with the eye of a man who knew how to make a map.

"It sures does!" he breathed. "That's the Lindon Land

Grant. You didn't quite get the lines right, Captain Fog, but I recognize the physical features of the map now. But the way this is drawn it makes the Grant appear to cover all our range and right up to the badlands.''

"Yeah," Dusty said quietly. "That's just how it looks."

Just at the moment Stone Hart entered from sending off his relief forces to the Gibbs' and Jones' places. He came forward and looked down at the map, seeing its significance.

"What do you make of it, Dusty?" he asked.

"I don't know for sure. But it'd take a trained man to make a map like this, wouldn't it?"

"Sure," Stone agreed. "This's been line-drawn from the original I'd say."

At last Lasalle found himself in a position to offer advice on something beyond the ken of the two Texans. He spent his service career in the Confederate Army Engineers and knew considerable about making maps.

"It was," he said. "The man who did it knew his work."

"A Government surveyor'd be able to do it I suppose?" Dusty asked.

"A well trained one would," Lasalle agreed.

"What're you thinking about, Dusty?" Stone asked, seeing the interest Dusty showed, although most people could have noticed no change in the small Texan's face or appearance.

"Just a hunch, Stone. I'll tell you more about it when I've met Clay."

He refused to say any more and Stone knew the futility of trying to get more out of him. After breakfast he still knew no more about Dusty's hunch but did not bother, he knew he would learn about it when Dusty had every detail worked out and not before.

"I'll head down to the herd and tell Waggles we're staying a spell," Stone said. "Johnny's gone ahead, should get them afore they head the cattle up."

They had finished breakfast and were preparing to start out. This time Mark would be riding with Dusty and they left warning that neither Lasalle nor Morg were to move far from the house and that they keep all weapons loaded.

"If they hit at you," Stone went on, after Dusty gave his grim warning, "get inside and fort up. Then make some smoke, burn rags or something, get smoke coming up from your chimney and we'll come a-running.''

"One thing, George," Dusty finished, turning his big paint stallion's head from the ranch. "Try and stick that map together for me.''

"Sure, Captain Fog," Lasalle promised. "If you reckon it's important.''

"I reckon that map's the middle of all this fuss," Dusty replied quietly. "Let's go, Mark. And don't worry if you hear riders coming up from the south on towards dark, George. It'll most likely be us.''

After his guests left, Lasalle went around his buildings with Morg at his side. They looked at the ragged hole left where the dynamite went off and Lasalle could not restrain a shudder, even though the other men had been up at the first hint of dawn to clear away the ghastly horror.

"We'll do like Captain Fog said, Morg," Lasalle stated. "Stay around the house and tidy things up today.''

"Sure, boss. Say, can I have a talk to you—about Freda and me?''

"I reckon you can," Lasalle replied. "Let's go to the barn. I wonder how Pop Jones and Ralph Gibbs'll find things today?''

At the Jones place a wagon stood before the door as Peaceful Gunn and his party rode up. The old man and the cowhand called Yance watched the trio of Wedge hands approach as they lifted chairs into the back of the canvas-topped wagon. "Howdy folks," greeted the man called Shaun, his tones showing his Irish birth. "Cap'n Fog sent us along to help you.''

"Knowed I shouldn't come here with this pair!" Peaceful moaned, eyeing the Colt the cowhand held. "Nobody'd trust me with villainous looking *hombres* like them at my back.''

"Sure and here's me a descendant of kings of auld Ireland being spoke ag'in by this evil-doer," replied Shaun, in his breezy brogue. "'Twas foolish to put all that gear into the wagon when we'll only have to be moving it out again.''

Then the Jones family and their hand started to smile. These were the men promised to lend a hand with the defense of the house. Pop looked right sprightly for a man who had been on the verge of losing his home. He took out a worn old ten gauge and set percussion caps on the nipples ready for use.

"Let's us get this lot back into the house," he suggested.

With eager hands to help the work was soon done. At Peaceful's suggestion they left the wagon standing outside, then Shaun turned on his Irish charm and got a very worried looking Ma Jones to smile.

"You don't sound like any Texan I ever heard," she said at last.

"I'm the only Texas-Irishman in the world," Shaun replied. "Can't you tell from me voice, a Texas drawl on top of a good Irish accent. Say, ma'am, you wouldn't know how to make an Irish stew, would you?"

On being assured that Ma not only could, but would, make an Irish stew, Shaun gave his full attention to making plans for the defence of the house.

Five hard looking men rode towards the Jones place shortly after noon. In the lead came Preacher Tring, sitting his horse uneasily for the Kid's birdshot onslaught had caught him in a most embarrassing position. This did not tend to make Tring feel any better disposed to life in general and the small ranch owners in particular.

He growled a low curse as he saw the wagon standing before the Jones' house and without a team. Clearly Pop Jones thought the Double K were playing kid games when they said get out. Right soon Pop would get a lesson.

Then the men put spurs to their horses and rode fast, coming down on the ranch and halting the mounts in a churned up dust cloud before the house. Tring dropped his hand towards his hip, meaning to draw and pour a volley into the house.

"Don't pull it, mister!" said a plaintive voice from the barn. "You'll like to scare me off."

All eyes turned to look in the direction of the speaker and all movement towards hardware ended. This might have been due to a desire to keep the nervous sounding man unafraid—or because all they could see plainly of him was the barrel of a Spencer rifle, its .52 calibre mouth yawning like a cave entrance at them.

"Is it the visitors we have, Peaceful?" a second voice inquired.

The wagon's canopy had drawn back and a Winchester

slanted at the Double K men, lined from the source of the Irish voice. Then a third man sauntered into view from the end of the house, also carrying a rifle, while a shotgun and a fourth rifle showed on either side of the open house door.

"Who are you?" Tring asked.

"We work here," Shaun replied. "Who are *you*?"

"Tell that pair of ole—!"

A bullet fanned Tring's hat from his head. The lever of Shaun's rifle clicked and the Double K men tried to keep their horses under control without also giving the idea they could reach their weapons.

"Just be keeping the civil tongue in your head, *hombre*!" Shaun warned. "And if you've no further business here, let's be missing you."

Tring had brought only four men with him as he did not expect any trouble in handling the Jones family and because the ranch crew had taken a mauling on their abortive attack at the Lasalle place. He knew he and the others had no chance of doing anything better than get shot to doll rags at the moment. However a second party of men were at the Gibbs place, attending to Mallick's orders. Tring decided to gather them in and return to the Jones house. When he came he would not leave a living soul at the house.

It was a good idea. Except that the other party were having troubles of their own.

They came on the Gibbs place, six of them, almost all the unwounded fighting strength of the Double K out on the business of clearing the two weakened small outfits out of the Panhandle country.

One of the men jerked his thumb towards where a tall, slim, studious young man leaned his shoulder against a corral post, clearly having been working on repairing the fence.

"Hey you!" he barked.

Doc Leroy looked up almost mildly. "Me sir?"

"Yeah, you! what in hell are you doing?"

"Fixing the fence," Doc answered.

From the house window Joyce watched with a quaking heart. She wondered why Rusty and Billy were not on hand to help Doc.

"Then start to pull it down!" ordered the man, a man she recognized from the previous visit.

"Now that'd be plump foolish," said Doc.

The man's hand dropped towards his gun and froze immobile a good inch from its butt.

Doc's right hand made a sight defying flicker, the ivory handled Colt came into it, lining on the man, the hammer drawn back.

"Just sit easy, *hombre*," Doc said, but his entire voice had changed. "And pray I don't let this hammer fall."

A footstep behind her brought Joyce swinging around. She found Rusty had entered from the back and was making for the front door, his rifle in his hands.

"Ole Doc sure is surprising, ain't he?" grinned Rusty and stepped out to lend his friend moral and actual support just as Billy emerged from the barn, complete with Henry rifle.

"Mrs. Gibbs!" Rusty said over his shoulder. "Come out here, ma'am and bring your scattergun." Joyce complied and Rusty indicated the men with the barrel of his rifle. "Any of them here yesterday?"

She stabbed up the shotgun, lining it on the man who did all the talking. "He was the one who shot Sam."

"Drop your guns, all of you!"

The words cracked from Rusty's mouth and the men obeyed. Then they were told to move to one side. Rusty put down his rifle and removed his gunbelt. He walked forward, going to the man Joyce indicated. His hands shot out, grabbing this man and hauling him from the saddle.

Rusty slammed the man on to the ground. His right fist shot into the man's stomach and ripped up a left as he doubled his man over. The man stood taller than Rusty but he never had a chance. He tried to fight back, but against Rusty's savage two handed attack he never stood a chance.

After a brutal five minute beating the man lay in a moaning heap on the floor and Rusty, nose bleeding and chest heaving, looked at Joyce.

"Any more of 'em here?" he asked.

"You leave them, boy," Doc answered coldly. "These gents have just volunteered to mend the corral."

The men most certainly had not intention of volunteering, but they were given no real choice in the matter. Under the guns of the three Wedge hands the men went to work. They might have hoped that Tring and his bunch would come to their aid but Doc put a block to such hopes.

"Happen anybody should come up and start throwing lead at us," he told the men, "we'll throw some back and you bunch'll get it first."

So, while hating fence building, or any other kind of work, the men hoped that Tring and his bunch would not come and try to rescue them.

Luckily for them Tring did not come. He started thinking after he left the Jones place and decided that Gibbs most likely had backing. The odds in the game were coming to a point where Tring no longer fancied them. Along with the others of his party he headed back to Double K and waited to hear what the Gibbs raiding party found. They did not return until after dark and came in looking sorry for themselves after working harder than any of them had done for years.

At dawn the following morning every man pulled out, heading for Barlock where they aimed to have a showdown with their boss, get such money as they could and pull out.

The Double K lay silent and peaceful after the men left. All the dead had been disposed of and the wounded taken into town, so only Sir James Keller and his daughter remained on the premises.

CHAPTER THIRTEEN

His Only Name Is Waco

THREE thousand head of longhorn Texas cattle wended their way across the range country. They kept in a long line, feeding as they moved. To prevent them from breaking out of their line, rode the trail hands, the point men at the head of the column, then the flank and swing men and at the back came the drag riders. Behind them moved the remuda and bringing up the rear two wagons, one driven by the cook, the other controlled by his louse.

The scene was one Dusty Fog and Mark Counter had seen many times. Yet they never grew tired of looking at it. This was the scene which brought money to Texas, allowed it to become the great and wealthy State it now was.

For a moment the two men sat and watched the trail hands riding the herd, horses jumping into a sprint to turn some steer which tried to avoid its destiny by breaking from the line. The steer would be turned back and another try the same move a few yards further on.

"Look restless," Dusty drawled.

"Maybe Clay ran into fuss," Mark replied. "There he is, the old cuss, right out front with Smiler and a kid I've never seen before."

Dusty had also noticed this. He studied the three riders about half a mile ahead of the herd. They saw Mark and Dusty at the same time and Clay Allison's hat came off to wave a greeting. Then both parties rode at a better pace towards each other.

Although they had not met for four years, Clay Allison looked little different, tall, slim, well dressed, even though trail dirty. He managed to keep his black moustache and short beard trimmed and neat, the matched guns at his sides were also clean and hung just right for a real fast draw. Smiler, tall, gaunt and looking more Indian than the Ysabel Kid, lounged in his saddle at his boss's side.

The boy at Clay's right took Dusty's attention, held it like a magnet. Not more than sixteen years old, but he still wore a brace of Army Colts in low hanging fast draw holsters. He had blond hair, a handsome face but looked cold and sullen. His clothes were not new, but they were good and serviceable.

Dusty bit down an exclamation for the boy looked much as had his brother Danny. Except that this kid looked meaner, the sort who either built himself the name as a real fast man with a gun—or found an early grave.

"Howdy Dusty, Mark," greeted Clay Allison. "Didn't expect to see you on this trail. You got a herd ahead?"

"Nope, but Stone Hart has," Dusty replied. "There's some fuss up ahead, Clay. Bad trouble. Let's pull off to one side and talk it out."

Waving his hand to one side Clay Allison nodded his agreement. They rode well clear of the herd, then swung down from their saddles. The youngster did not follow immediately but sat his horse for a moment watching the approaching herd.

"Who's the boy, Clay?" Dusty asked, nodding towards the youngster.

"His only name is Waco," Allison replied. "Been with me for nigh on six months now. I met up with him down in Tascosa. He was in a bar and all set to take on half a dozen Yankee soldiers. So I cut in and helped him. Been with me ever since. That boy's fast, Dusty, real fast. And he knows it."

At that moment the boy whose only name was Waco rode to join the four men as they stood under the shade of a cottonwood tree's branches. The horses were allowed to stand and graze to one side and Allison nodded to the herd as they passed.

"They've been so spooked up for the past few days that you have to ride a mile from 'em to cough or spit."

Dusty grunted his sympathy. He knew how uncertain the behaviour of a bunch of longhorn cattle could be. They might go through a howling gale or a thunderstorm without turning a hair, or they might just as easily spook and take to running at their own shadows. It all depended on how they felt.

"What's ahead, Dusty?" asked Allison.

"Wire."

"WIRE!"

Three voices said the word in a single breath. Clay Allison, Smiler and Waco each spat the word out as if it burned their mouths.

"Who strung it?" asked Smiler.

"Now that's a problem," Dusty admitted. "It's across the narrows on the old Lindon Land Grant."

"Lindon never block the trail," Smiler went on, speaking more then he had spoken in months.

"Lindon sold out to an Englishman," Mark replied, watching the boy called Waco and paying particular attention to the way Waco studied himself and Dusty. "I reckon Dusty's not satisfied that the new owner's behind the wire-stringing though."

Dusty glanced at his big *amigo* and grinned. It looked like he couldn't fool Mark or keep his thoughts from the big cowhand after all these years. Before Dusty could make a reply to Mark's words, Waco put his say-so in.

"This Englishman got you scared, or something?" he asked.

"Or something, boy," Dusty answered, knowing youngsters of Waco's type.

Yet somehow Dusty got the idea there was better than the makings of a fast-gun killer in the boy. The face, while sullen, looked intelligent and did not carry lines of dissipation. Not that it would stay that way long. Clay Allison might be a rancher, but Dusty knew the kind of men he hired. Good hands with cattle, but a wild onion crew form the Pecos, men who handled their guns better than average and liked to show their skill. A boy growing and spending his formative years in such company had one foot on the slope and the devil dragging at his other leg.

"Boy!" Waco hissed.

"Choke off, Waco!" Clay snapped.

Waco relapsed into silence, watching Dusty now with cold eyes. He had been an orphan almost since birth, his name came from people calling him the Waco-orphaned baby on the wagon train where his parents died. In time it became shortened to but one name, Waco. He had been reared by settlers, but never took their name even though they treated him with such kindness and love as could be shared for they had nine children of their own. He grew in a raw land and carried a gun form the day he was old enough to tote one. Now he rode for Clay Allison's CA spread and he didn't let any man talk down to him, especially not a short growed runt like that cowhand talking to Clay. It surprised Waco considerable that Clay would waste time in talking with such a small and insignificant man.

"What're you down here for, Dusty?" Clay went on.

"I'd like you to bring your herd to a halt for a day or so and come up trail with me. Bring a few of the boys. I've got Stone Hart along. Between us we ought to be able to wind this up without starting a war."

"Wind hell!" Clay barked. "That wire's got to go and I say it ought to go around the feller who strung it's neck."

"He's got around twenty guns backing him," Dusty answered. "And there's a whole slew of folks up that way, small ranchers, who can't stand a war fighting over their land."

Whatever his faults, and they were many, Clay Allison respected the property and persons of people less fortunate in the matter of wealth than himself; as long as they did not encroach on his holdings or make trouble for him, which the small ranchers up here did not. He nodded his head, seeing what Dusty said to be the truth. He also knew Dusty would not be back here unless he had some definite plan. However he did not feel happy about being too far from his herd while they acted so spooked.

"Tell me about it as we ride," he suggested.

"You sure want some help," Waco suddenly put, in facing Dusty.

"How do you mean?" asked Dusty.

"Come high tailing it down here to ask Clay to fight your fight for you."

"That's enough, boy!" Dusty's voice took a warning note.

"Don't call me boy!" Waco snapped. "I'm a man grown with these guns on."

"Then try acting like one."

The words met with the wrong reaction on Waco's part. His right hand dropped towards his gun. He did not make it.

Dusty caught the warning flicker in the youngster's eyes, his left hand crossed his body, fetching out the Colt from the right holster, lining it with the hammer drawn back under his thumb. For a long moment he stood like that, the others not moving either. Waco stood still, not entirely scared but numb and unbelieving. He thought he was fast with a gun, but this small man did not just stop at being fast. Somehow it did not matter to Waco if lead smashed into him. He had made his play and failed, he knew the penalty for failure.

With his thumb trembling on the gun hammer Dusty waited and watched. Then suddenly he lowered the Colt's hammer, spun the weapon on his finger, holstered it and turned to walk to his paint horse.

Letting out his breath in a long sigh Clay Allison followed, then Smiler also turned and walked away. Only Mark and Waco stood where they had dismounted to hold their talk, under the shade of a cottonwood tree.

"He didn't have the guts to drop the hammer!" Waco sneered. "The d—"

Mark's big hand clamped on to the youngster's shirt, lifting him from his feet and slamming him back into a tree as if he weighed no more than a baby. Then Mark thrust his face up close to Waco's.

"Listen good to me, you hawg-stupid kid. Only one thing saved you from being killed or wounded bad. Dusty's brother was killed a few months back. You look a lot like him, except that he was a man, not just some trigger-fast-and-up-from-Texas kid."

With a contemptuous gesture Mark thrust Waco from him. Then he turned to go and collect his horse. Waco's face flushed with rage, his hand lifted over the butts of his guns.

"Turn around!" he snapped.

Mark turned, noting the stance. "What's on your mind, boy?"

"Nobody lays hands on me and lives to boast about it."

They faced each other, hands over the butts of their guns. The other three rode away, not knowing what went on behind them for their attention rested on the cattle.

Just what started the stampede they never discovered. It could have been any of a number of things, or none of them. It most likely stemmed from the ornery nature of the Texas

Longhorn steer, a breed of cattle never noted for the stability or gentleness of its behavior.

Whatever the cause, one moment the herd moved along in its normal manner. The next saw every steer bellowing and leaping forward, galloping into wild stampede which swept aside the hands, made them draw clear or be run down.

"Stampede!" roared Clay Allison. "All hands and the cook!"

The old range cry brought every man forward at a gallop. Now they must try to reach the point of the herd, turn it, make the leaders swing around until they joined on the rear of the column, then keep them running in a circle until they tired and came to a halt. Only it would not be as easy as all that. Those wild-eyed racing steers would not willingly turn.

Clay's shout and the noise of the stampede reached Mark and Waco's ears. To give him credit Waco dropped his aggressive pose even before Mark relaxed and the youngster made his horse's saddle before Mark reached the bloodbay. Their difference of opinion was forgotten. Only one thing mattered now. To ride and help turn the herd.

Racing his horse at a tangent Waco came boiling down on the herd's point ahead of the other men. He urged the horse on, cutting down so as to try and slam into the lead steer and make it swing. The horse he rode knew its business, had been trained for cattle work. It ran well, then put its foot in a gopher hole and went down. Waco heard the terrified scream of the horse as he flew over its head. His instincts as a horseman saved him, allowed him to land on his feet, running. Then he stopped and turned, the herd headed straight at him now, the leaders seeing a hated man-thing on his feet and at their mercy instead of on a horse where he was their master.

The youngster turned, he saw his horse struggling to rise, terror and pain in its rolling eyes for its leg had broken. His right hand dipped and brought out the Army Colt to throw a bullet into the horse's head and end its terror and misery. Then he turned and tried to run but high heeled cowhand boots were never meant for running on and a longhorn steer could keep a horse hard-pressed to catch it.

Nearer came the steers, their horns, which could go to a six foot spread, lowered and ready to rip into him. Waco knew it would be no use turning and trying to shoot his way clear. He

found a situation where his skill with a gun stood for nothing
and all he could do was run.

"Waco!"

A single shout reached his ears, ringing above the noise of
the herd. He twisted his head and saw a paint stallion bearing
down on him. He saw the small man who he dismissed as
nobody, and nothing and who he tried to draw on, cutting in
ahead of the cattle, coming across the widening front of
horns. Waco knew that if Dusty slowed down the herd would
be on them before they could make a move to escape the rush.

Dusty knew the danger also. He measured the distance between the running youngster and the onrushing herd. This
would be tricky, one false move, a wrong step on the part of
the seventeen hand paint and they would all be under the
hooves of the stampeding herd.

Bending low in the saddle Dusty prepared to grab Waco's
waist band. He gave quick, tense instructions.

"Get set, boy. When I grab you, make a jump. I'll sling you
across the back of the saddle. Then hang on with all you've
got."

Waco heard the words, felt the presence of the big paint at
his side. Then a hand grabbed him by the pant's belt and he
felt himself heaved up. He had not expected such strength, his
feet left the ground and he felt himself dragged towards the
paint's back. Then he grabbed the cantle of the saddle to help
out, hauling himself to hang across the horse's rump. The
double girths of the rig took the strain and stood it. Waco
writhed, he felt a horn brush his leg, then the paint ran the
gauntlet of the herd, cutting to one side of them. The leaders
did not aim to be so easily cheated of their prey. They swung
after the paint, with its near helpless bundle hanging over the
rump and slowing it.

Racing his big bloodbay stallion ahead of any of the others,
Mark brought it full at the lead steer. Seeing the huge horse
tearing at him, the steer started to swing slightly. Mark gave it
no chance to reverse towards Dusty but crowded in once more.
Clay Allison came up, followed by his brothers Ben and Jack.
Between them the four men started to swing the stampede
around, away from where Dusty brought his horse to a halt
and lowered Waco to the ground. He did not leave the
youngster for there was still the danger of a stray longhorn

coming up and the longhorn did not fear a man afoot.

"They've got 'em!" Dusty said with satisfaction. "Making 'em do a merry-go-round. That'll slow 'em down."

Waco did not reply. He looked at the small man, only he no longer saw Dusty as being small. He knew he owed the other man his life, not once, but twice. Dusty could have killed him back there when he tried to draw. Then at the risk of his own life Dusty came to rescue him. This was a kind of man Waco had never met before and did not know what to make of. Clearly Dusty gave no thought to the incident back under the cottonwood, his full attention being on the herd.

They watched the circle made, and the steers began to slow, being kept in a circle all the time. Slowly the movement came to an end but the hands continued to ride their circle.

Clay Allison and Mark swung from the herd, riding to where Dusty and Waco stood waiting.

"You came close to being the late Waco, boy," Mark said.

"Yeah," agreed Clay. "I never thought to see you alive when your hoss went down. Reckon you owe Dusty something."

Slowly Waco turned, his eyes on Dusty.

"I reckon I do. I'm sorry for what happened back there Dusty."

A smile flickered on Dusty's face. He knew what the apology meant to Waco. It had been torn from him for he had never felt he owed any man a thing, now he owed Dusty his life.

"That's all right, boy. You did the man's thing back there when you shot that hoss rather than leave it to be stampeded under by the herd. You might have got clear with no trouble if you hadn't."

"It was my hoss, never let me down. I couldn't let it down at the end."

Smiles came to faces of the watching men. Then Clay pointed back to the remuda which approached them.

"You've got your pick of any hoss in the bunch, boy. Go take it."

A grin came to Waco's face, softening the sullen expression. Until this moment Clay never referred to him as anything but his own name. It looked like Dusty had stuck him with a fresh title. Somehow he did not mind. The word "boy" was now spoken in a different manner. Now Dusty regarded him as a boy who would one day grow into a man.

"I'll lend you a hand to get your saddle out, boy," Mark drawled. "Come on."

There were good horses in Clay Allison's remuda. One of them caught Waco's eye. He took up the rope from the saddle he'd laid on the ground. With a quick whirl he sent a hooley-ann loop flipping out to settle on the neck of a big young paint stallion, a seventeen hand beauty as yet untrained in cattle work. This horse he led out. It had been three saddled, ridden the three times which a bronc-buster considered all that was necessary before handing the horse into the remuda and since then little ridden. Clay brought it along to test out anybody who wanted to ride it, only Waco aimed to be the only man who ever did.

"You've picked a mean one there, boy," drawled Mark, on whom the implication of the choice was not lost. "He's got a belly full of bed-springs that need taking out before he'll be any use."

"Then I'm going to have to take them out," Waco replied.

Dusty and Clay watched the herd settle down before they offered to do anything else. Clay sat his horse and cursed the fool steers which had run off a fair amount of beef in the stampede.

"Keep 'em here and range feed for a spell," Dusty suggested. "Two, three days on this buffalo grass'll put the meat on them again. And by that time, happen you go along with me, we'll have this wire trouble fixed and the narrows opened again."

"I'll go along."

"Leave the herd here, with Ben and Jack, get half a dozen or more men you can rely on not to start a shooting match unless they have to, ride to the Lasalle place, and we'll pick Stone up on the way. Then I'll tell all of you what I aim to do."

It said much for Clay Allison's faith in Dusty that he agreed to this without inquiring what Dusty's plans might be. He felt fully satisfied that Dusty not only had a plan but could also see that same plan through given a bit of aid.

Calling his brother Ben over, Clay told of Dusty's arrangements. Ben listened and gave his agreement. Then he jerked

his thumb along to the remuda where Waco and Mark were
saddling the big paint.

"Waco sure picked the beauty this time," he said. "Told
me you said he could have hand-choice of the remuda and he
wanted the paint, so I told him to go ahead. Why in hell did he
pick that hoss out of the rest?"

A grin twisted Clay's lips and he glanced at Dusty's big
horse which stood grazing to one side.

"I wonder why?" he said.

Three times the paint threw Waco, but each time he got up
and mounted again. He showed he could really handle a horse
and the fourth time on he stuck there until the horse gave in.
Not until then did he join the other men at the fire and took
the mug of coffee offered by the cook. His eyes were on Dusty
all the time, his ears working to catch every word Dusty said.
Not until then did he fully realize who Dusty was for nobody
had introduced him.

After the meal Clay selected six men, including Waco, to
ride with them and see about moving the wire.

"We're r'aring to go, Cap'n Fog," said one of the men.

"Then un-rear!" Dusty snapped. "There's a time to talk
and a time to fight. We'll try talk first."

"Hell they ain't but a bunch of hired guns, way you told us,
Dusty," Waco objected.

"You're just as dead no matter who puts the lead into you,
boy," Dusty answered. "And a lot of innocent folks might get
hurt at the same time."

Usually Waco would have scoffed at the idea of worrying
about other people. This time he did not. He sat back and
waited to hear what the others said on the subject.

"We'll do whatever you say, Dusty," Clay stated firmly.
"Then if talk don't work we can always try making war."

The Lasalle house had a crowd in it after dark that evening,
not counting the Allison hands who lounged around outside,
letting their boss make the talk while they ate some good fix-
ings.

In the dining-room Dusty, Mark, Clay Allison, Stone Hart
and Waco sat with Lasalle and Morg. The girl came in and
joined her father after serving a meal from the supplies the CA
crew brought along. They had barely got down to business
when Johnny Raybold arrived, bringing word that although

visited by the Double K men the Jones' and Gibbs' houses were fine and without a worry in the world.

"Never seed ole Peaceful looking so miserable," he concluded, to show that all really was well.

"I thought I'd send him visiting to earn his pay," Stone remarked.

"I sure earned it," Johnny grinned. "Mrs. Gibbs done made a pie for the boys, had it all a-cooling on the window. Only it's not there any more." Here Johnny rolled his eyes in ecstasy and rubbed his stomach. "Man, that Mrs. Gibbs sure is one good cook. Not that you-all aint, Miss Freda."

This latter came as he caught an accusing gleam in Freda's eyes and remembered visiting the house and praising her cooking.

"I bet you say that to all the cooks," she replied.

"I do, I do. But I sure don't want to meet up with Rusty, Doc'n Billy for a spell, not 'til they get over losing their pie."

"Now that's a shame. That sure is a shame," Dusty drawled. "Because you're headed over there right now, then on to Jones'. I want them here with their wagons in the morning so we can take them into town for supplies."

"Sure," Johnny replied, secure in the knowledge that no reprisals could be taken on him while he rode on urgent business. "I'll tell them."

"Just one man with each wagon," Dusty went on. "The other two stay on and guard the house."

"Yo!" Johnny replied and left the room.

"What's your plan, Dusty?" Clay asked.

"Easy enough. We're going into town tomorrow in force. And we're serving notice on the Double K bunch that they get out of town. After that I'm getting some questions answered by Mr. Mallick, the Land Agent, whether he wants to answer or not."

"And after that?" Stone put in.

"I want to get this fence business ended one way or the other. I aim to run Elben out of Barlock so the Double K doesn't have the backing of the law. Then, if I have to I'm going to see Keller and show him the error of his ways."

CHAPTER FOURTEEN

The Freeing Of Barlock

THE town of Barlock lay sleepily under the early morning sun. Few people walked the streets. In the office of the Land Agent an emergency meeting had been called. Mallick sat at his desk, sullen and scowling. Jackieboy Disraeli sat in a chair with a pout like a petulant schoolgirl on his face. To one side, by the door, stood Knuckles, leaning against the wall and looking about as intelligent as the wooden planks behind him. Before the desk stood Elben, and a man from the Double K, a hired gun who had slipped away early in order to have a chance at making some money at the expense of his friends.

"So you came here with a warning?" asked Mallick, in a mocking tone as he watched the man's face.

"Yeah."

"Why?"

"I reckoned it'd be worth something for you to know what Tring's fixing to do," replied the gunman.

Mallick looked at the man, and his voice still stayed mocking. "I see. So Tring and the rest are coming here to make us pay them for work they botched and couldn't complete."

"Yeah."

"And you thought you would warn us out of the goodness of your heart?" piped Disraeli, also watching the man.

"I reckoned it'd be worth at least a hundred dollars for you to know," answered the man, throwing a contemptuous look at the fancy dressed man.

The sudden anger which came to Disraeli's face should have warned the man of his danger, but he was more interested in talking himself into money, then getting away from town before the others arrived. Disraeli snapped his fingers and pointed at the man.

With a slow, almost beast-like snarl Knuckles left his place. He moved faster than one might have thought possible for so bulky a man. The gunman heard Knuckles and started to turn, his hand dropping towards the butt of his gun. Knuckles drove out a big fist, throwing it with all his power. Like the arrival of a thunderbolt it smashed into the side of the man's head as he turned. He flew across the room, his head snapped over and hanging at an unnatural angle. The others watched him hurl into the wall, hit it and slide down.

Crossing the room, Elben bent over and looked down at the man. Then he lifted scared eyes to Disraeli and Mallick. The Land Agent stood staring, but Disraeli remained in his seat, sadistic pleasure etched on his face.

"He's dead!" Elben said. "His neck's broke."

"So?"

There was challenge in Disraeli's one-word reply, mockery too, for Disraeli liked nothing better than to see stronger men who might have treated him with derision and mockery but cowered before the awful might of Knuckles. He watched Elben, seeing the marshal's eyes flicker to Knuckles who ignored the man he had struck down and killed and was now leaning against the wall again.

"I only told you," Elben answered. "What do you want us to do with him?"

"That's for you to decide," Mallick answered. "It was self defence on Knuckles' part. Now get down to your office and come back in a couple of hours with some of your men and clear that carrion out of here."

After the door closed on Elben's departing back, Mallick and Disraeli exchanged glances.

"I think we're finished here, don't you?" Disraeli asked.

Mallick nodded. "I think we are. What next?"

"We run. I have a friend in New York who can get us on a boat for Europe and we can disappear into some big city if we find that the law is after us. That is one advantage to being of my race, Mallick, the brotherhood of my people will shield us from the Gentiles."

"And what about me?" asked Mallick.

"You too, old friend. A little more money might help us though."

They exchanged glances. Both had money from their

scheme, although not as much as at first expected. The hiring of gunmen took much of the cream from their profits but the same men had been a necessity.

"Keller has the money to complete the purchase," Mallick remarked. "And for his running costs as he calls them. And he had a collection of jewelry, as you told me when you first put this idea to me. He'll be at the ranch, alone except for his daughter and with that bad ankle won't be any a problem. He'll never suspect anything until too late."

An evil gleam came to Disraeli's eyes. "Yes that's the idea!" he said, slapping his hands together like an excited girl. "I'll have revenge for my brother and see that accursed Sir James Keller suffer."

"Let's destroy all the papers on the Lindon Land Grant, and do a thorough job this time!" Mallick said. "Then we'll get the wagon, the money, and go to the Double K."

Half an hour later only the ashes of burned paper lay in the waste-paper basket, the body of the gunman sprawled by the wall. The doors were locked, that at the front bolted also for Mallick's party left by the rear.

They called at the saloon where Disraeli emptied his office safe, took all the money and the deeds to the business from it. Then, after making sure that no incriminating papers remained the two men went to where Knuckles had a fast two horse carriage awaiting them. They left town and took cover in a wood while Tring and his men rode by, then they headed across the range in the direction of the Double K.

When he found the birds had flown Tring cursed savagely. A look over the painted lower half of the Land Agent's office windows showed him the room held only the body of a man who would have sold them out. The safe door hung open and clearly Mallick was gone. So had his partner Jackieboy Disraeli, when they came to the saloon. A boot sent his office door flying open but once more the Double K had arrived too late.

"We'll take it out of here boys," Tring said waving a hand towards the saloon. "And anything more we need this stinking lil town's going to give us."

His plan only partially succeeded. The men headed for the bar where scared bartenders poured drinks and emptied the till for Tring and the hired gunmen. They drank and then one of the men standing by a window and watching the street, gave a warning shout.

Silence fell on the room. They heard the sound of hooves, many hooves and gathered to see who came to town. Mutters of surprise and fear rose from amongst the men as they recognized the men who led the well armed party into town.

"There's Dusty Fog and Mark Counter!" one man said. "We never touched either of them when we hit Lasalle's."

"Naw. They weren't staying in the house 'cause they was scared neither," another went on, putting forth the reason one faction of the raiding party offered for Dusty and Mark not coming after them in revenge for the attack on Lasalle's. They was waiting for help."

"And they got it!" a third put in. "That's Clay Allison and Stone Hart up front and some of their boys along."

"They coming in here?" asked a fourth man, casting an eye on the rear door.

"Nope, going through."

They formed quite a party, coming down the main street. The four men in the lead each famous in his own right. Behind them came the Gibbs and Jones' wagons, driven by the women and flanked by men. Stone had called a further four men from his herd, bringing the fighting force to fourteen, but they were fourteen who might have made a troop of cavalry think twice about attacking.

"There's the stores, Clay," Dusty said. "Get to it."

In his store Matt Roylan looked at the two gunhung deputies who now lounged at the counter and decimated his profits by their constant dipping into cracker barrel or candy jar.

"How the hell does your boss expect me to make a living with you scaring trade off?" he asked.

"Whyn't you go and ask him?" answered one of the men, then looked towards the door.

Horses and a wagon had halted outside. Then boots thudded on to the sidewalk and up to the door. It opened and two tall men stepped inside, two men with low hanging guns, although one of them did not look more than sixteen years old.

"The name's Clay Allison," said the bearded man and jerked a thumb to where Ma Jones stood by her wagon. "The lady aims to buy supplies and I'm here to see she gets them. Understand?''

The two deputies understood. So did Roylan. He removed his apron, walked around the end of the counter and shot out a hand to grip each collar of the gunmen. With spirit and delight he hustled the two men across his business premises, doing what his heart craved to do ever since they first came here. He heaved the two astonished deputies through the door, ran them to the edge of the sidewalk and hurled them off. With a delighted grin Roylan looked down at them.

"That was gentle!" he said. "The next of you shows his face in here gets it damaged!"

One of the deputies sat up, mouthing curses. His hand went to his side, to grip the butt of his gun, eyes glowing hate at Roylan's back as the storekeeper turned to Ma Jones.

Waco lunged through the door, his right hand Colt coming clear and lining on the man.

"Loose it!" he snapped. "Then on your feet and find a hoss. The next time I see you I'll shoot."

Watching this Clay Allison felt puzzled and then smiled. Waco would have shot the man without a chance had this happened yesterday. Waco also felt surprised at the change in his outlook. His first instinct had been to shoot, to send lead into the gunman. Then, at the last instant, he held his hand. He knew Dusty Fog had said no killing unless it became necessary. He could not see Dusty, or Mark, wanting truck with a fool trigger-fast-and-up-from-Texas kid who cut down a man in cold blood.

So Waco watched the man get to his feet, then kept the two deputies under observation as they walked away. He stood aside and let Roylan and Ma Jones enter the store.

"I had to do it, Ma," Roylan said. "So did Banker O'Neil. They threatened his wife and family unless he went along with them. It's over now."

She nodded. "It looks that way."

Mrs. Gibbs traded with the other store. She found that her escort would consist of Stone Hart, Rusty Willis and Peaceful Gunn. They made for the store where Peaceful and Rusty insisted on entering first, to sort of watch things and kind of make sure the deputies didn't get too festive when Mrs. Gibbs entered. This was Rusty's idea. Peaceful moaned about it being safer inside than on the streets where already Dusty's men were letting out their wild cowhand yells, firing guns into the air and doing all they could to produce the local law.

In the store Jake Billings leaned his old frame on the counter and glowered at the pair of deputies, one of whom lit his third free cigar from Jake's private stock.

"You pair's supposed to be deputies," he said. "Whyn't you get out there afore those cowhands ropes the town and hauls it back to the Old Trail with them."

"Not us. We're special deputies," replied one of the men, his face bearing marks of Mark Counter's big fists.

They looked at the door as Rusty Willis and Peaceful Gunn entered. The two cowhands separated, crossing the store to halt one by each deputy. Peaceful removed his hat and held it in his right hand, mopping his brow with a large red handkerchief and letting his moustache droop in an abject manner.

"Them rowdies out there," he said in his usual mournful and whining tone for such an occasion. "They're causing so much fuss that I'll just get me some t'baccy and light out afore the marshal comes and jails everybody in sight."

If anything could have lulled the suspicions of the two deputies, Peaceful words were most likely to succeed. Neither of the hard-cases gave him another glance. The second deputy looked at Rusty who stood by him and took up a heavy skillet.

"Chow asked me to get him one of these," he drawled, looking at the deputy. "You reckon this'n'd be all right?"

"How the hell would I know?" snapped the deputy, then looked to where Stone and Mrs. Gibbs came through the door. "What do you want?"

"The lady's here for her supplies," Stone answered.

"Then she can get the hell out of—!" began the deputy by Peaceful.

His speech did not end. Peaceful moved at a speed which amazed Joyce, when she thought of his usual lethargic movements. His hat lashed back, full into the man's face. Two pounds of prime J. B. Stetson could hurt when lashed around with the full power of a brawny arm. The gunman's hand, almost on his gun butt, missed and he gave forth a startled, pain-filled yell.

The second man sent his hand flying towards his gun and almost made it. At his side Rusty gripped the heavy skillet by the handle and swung it sideways, using the edge like an axe blade against the man's stomach. With a croaking cry of pain the gunman doubled over, holding his middle. Up lifted the pan to come down with a resounding and very satisfying clang, on to the temptingly offered head. Billings let out a whoop of delight, but the gunman gave only a moan to show his disapproval of Rusty's actions.

With tears in his eyes, the deputy Peaceful assailed with his hat dropped a hand towards the butt of his gun. Steel glinted in Peaceful's hand, the bowie knife which mostly rode at the peace lover's left side, now lay in his hand, its clipped point driving at the man's stomach, Joyce let out a gasp of fear for she expected to see the deputy drop writhing in agony and spurting blood on the floor.

At the last instant Peaceful changed his aim slightly, the knife rose and then cut down, the razor sharp lower edge ripping through the leather of the man's gunbelt causing it to drop. The deputy's hand clawed air for his holster now hung mouth down by the pigging thong and his gun lay at his feet.

"I'm a man of peace, I am!" warned Peaceful and cut again, this time through the gunman's waist band causing him to grab hurriedly at his pants. "And if I sees you again after you go through that door I'll prove it!"

Taking the hint, and holding his pants up at the same time, the deputy headed past Joyce and out through the door. She watched him go and smiled a little. It appeared that the hardcase Double K were not as hard as she at first imagined.

She knew why her friends acted in the way they did. Stone Hart might be accepted as a master trail boss, but his name did not carry the same weight as Clay Allison's in gun fighting circles. So Stone and his men arranged to take care of the deputies before announcing their presence, or at least to make sure that the two deputies could be rendered harmless by having Rusty and Peaceful on hand before Stone brought Joyce intot he building.

"About these supplies, friend?" Stone asked.

Billings grinned. "You can have them, Joyce. I didn't dare go again Mallick until I had some backing. But I got it now. What do you want?"

"It telled you we ought to've gone round!" Peaceful wailed. "I—"

Joyce spun to face him and stabbed an accusing finger at his face. "You're a fake!" she yelled. "And if you ever mention peace and quiet to me again I'll drag you east by the ear and make sure you get some."

The threat brought a heart-rending sigh from Peaceful. "There," he told Rusty miserably. "For this here lady I forget me true and beautiful nature, and that's all the thanks I get."

Since the arrival of the Texans there had been a steady departure from the Jackieboy Saloon. Men who took pay for their fighting ability drifted out, mounted their horses and rode out of town. The word had passed around that Barlock would be unhealthy for any hired gun who took pay from Double K and they aimed to stay healthy as long as they could.

One of the men who went was Preacher Tring. Unlike the others he did not have his horse before the saloon, but left it saddled and ready down by the civic pound. He left the saloon by its rear entrance, having an idea that his prominence in matters of the Double K, including the attack of the Lasalle house and attempted dynamiting, would put him high on the list of those most wanted by Mark Counter and Dusty Fog.

Tring went to the civic pound, a walled corral in which stood the horses of Elben and his deputies. His own horse waited at the rear and he passed around to the rear of the corral. Just as he was about to mount and shake the dust of Barlock for ever from his feet, he saw a man come around the side of the town marshal's office and halt standing facing the rear door of the building.

A hiss of satisfaction left Tring's llps. The man was Dusty Fog. More he clearly did not suspect Tring's presence or he would never have been foolish enough to present his back in such a tempting manner.

Never again would Tring have such a chance of killing Dusty Fog. The small Texan's back was to him, his attention fixed on the rear door of the marshal's office. Tring's horse stood saddled and only needed mounting for a rapid departure to safer pastures once he sent lead between Dusty's shoulders. Ever since Dusty drove him from the Double K, Tring had nursed hatred and swore he would be revenged. Now it seemed he would be given his chance.

Not suspecting the danger behind him, Dusty Fog stood watching the rear door of the town marshal's office. He took no part in the general freeing of Barlock and clearance of the Double K hired guns. For himself, Dusty reserved the duty, if not the pleasure, of handling the matter of Mallick's tame lawman.

Dusty never made any move without good reason. His reasons for removing Elben were simple. The man wore a law badge. He might not have been elected by true democratic principles but he held the badge and while he wore it he had certain rights and privileges. So Dusty aimed to see Elben and use moral persuasion, of his own style, to make Elben resign from office. In other words Elben was to be offered the chance of resigning, or being resigned forcibly. Dusty did not intend allowing Mallick the protection of a law badge when they met and discussed the matter of the Lindon Land Grant.

The office door opened and Elben emerged carrying a saddle and looking back across the room. Dusty knew at what Elben looked. On the front porch Mark Counter stood waiting and Elben wondered when the blond giant would come after him to take reprisals for the attack upon his person on Mark's last visit to town.

Whatever his other faults, and they were many, Elben counted himself as being smart enough to know when to yell "calf rope" and get clear of danger. He had seen the eviction of his deputies from the stores and the departure of Double K men so knew his term of office was due for a sudden termination at the hands of the enraged citizenry of Barlock.

With that thought in mind Elben took his saddle which he kept in his room. He emptied the office safe of various little trinkets and keepsakes presented by people around town, including the donations made by various sources to his election campaign funds. These he stuffed into a saddlebag, took up the saddle and headed for the back door, aiming to collect a horse and ride out.

"Going someplace?"

The words brought Elben around in a startled turn. He stood with the saddle in his right hand, his left hovering over the butt of his gun. Then he stiffened and his hovering hand froze for he recognized the small man standing before him.

"Yeah, Cap'n," he said. "I'm going someplace."

He thought of the money in his saddlebags. Money extorted from various people around town. To be caught with it was likely to wind him up in jail for a fair time and he didn't want such a thing to happen. Yet he did not see how he could avoid it.

At that moment Elben saw Tring sneaking along the side of the corral behind Dusty. This would be his chance for Tring held a gun and clearly aimed to use it. Elben watched the man raising the gun, licked his lips with the flickering tip of his tongue and prepared to take a hand. He could get off a shot into Dusty Fog even as Tring fired, showing his heart to be in the right place. Then he and Tring would be free to make good their escape. For a share of the loot Tring would carry his saddle while he rode bareback until they had time to halt and get the saddle on Elben's mount.

Elben tensed slightly as Tring aimed the gun. At the same moment he heard a voice yell one word.

"Dusty!"

A tall, blond youngster burst into view around the corner of the office, his hands fanning down towards the butts of his guns. Instantly everything burst into wild and sudden action.

Hearing the yell and seeing the danger, Tring turned his gun and fired at the newcomer, his bullet fanning by Waco's cheek. Even as he did so. Dusty flung himself backwards and to one side, hands crossing and fetching out his matched guns. At the same instant Elben let his saddle fall and clawed out his right hand gun to take a hand in the game.

Dusty's matched guns roared, slightly less than three-quarters of a second after his first move. He threw his lead at Tring, shooting to prevent the man correcting his aim and cutting Waco down. In doing so Dusty put his own life in peril for he had his back to Elben and the ex-town marshal's gun was already sliding clear.

A warning flicker caught the corner of Waco's eye, brought his attention to Dusty's danger. He ignored Tring, ignored the fact that the next bullet from the gunman might hit him. He aimed to save Dusty Fog's life even if he died doing it.

Even as Dusty's lead smashed into Tring, rocking him over into the corral fence and sending him down, Waco shot Elben, shot him in the head, aiming for an instant kill to prevent him being able to trigger off even one shot.

"You fool kid," Dusty said quietly, but there was admiration in his voice. "Why in hell didn't you put lead into Tring?"

"Figured you could handle him, and that *hombre* behind you sure didn't aim to play spit-balls," Waco replied.

One look at Elben told Dusty the marshal offered no danger to him now. He heard running feet as men came to investigate the shooting. then he holstered his guns and walked towards Waco.

"You risked Tring killing you to save me," he said, speaking quietly.

"And you hauled me out from under that stampede," Waco replied. "Figured to get even, but," he looked at where Tring lay sprawled by the corral, "you're still one up on me."

Mark reached the scene first, coming with guns in his hands. He holstered the weapons, looked at the scene before him and read its implications. He had seen Waco leave the store and pass between the two buildings, disobeying Dusty's orders, but could also see that likely Waco's disobedience saved Dusty's life.

"Why'd you come here?" he asked.

"Me'n Clay'd done our lil piece down at the store and I figured to see how this here moral persuasion worked," Waco replied with a grin.

"You did the right thing, boy," drawled Mark and slapped Waco on the shoulder. "For once."

A grin came to Waco's face. He doubted if he could have been given greater praise than that.

"Let's get to the Land Agent's office, Mark," Dusty said. "These gents here can attend to the bodies."

After unlocking the rear door with a powerful kick from Mark's right leg, Dusty led the way into the office. Mark and Waco followed on his heels and they stood behind Dusty, looking at the body by the wall, then at the charred remains of many papers lying in the waste-paper basket.

"Looks like we got here too late," Dusty said.

Mark did not reply. He went to the body and looked down at it, seeing the bruise left by a fist and the way the neck hung. It had taken a man with exceptional strength to deliver such a blow and one man sprang to Mark's mind.

One thought led to another, Mark's nostrils quivered as he sniffed at the sickly scent which still hung in the office.

"Remember that first time we came to see Mallick, Dusty?" he asked. "We smelled this same scent in here then. Thought it might be some calico cat Mallick had been entertaining. Only I know it wasn't. That fat little swish* who owns the Jackieboy Saloon uses it. And the trained ape he had with him was strong enough to have bust this feller's neck with a punch.''

''Best go along to the saloon then,'' Dusty replied.

As Dusty expected, the saloon's owner had departed with Mallick and nobody appeared to know where they had gone. However, on going outside to see that everything in the streets was peaceful and the Double K men cleared out of town, Dusty met Matt Roylan. After the storekeeper thanked him for freeing Barlock from the clutches of the gunmen, Roylan remarked that he had seen Mallick, Disraeli and Knuckles making a hurried departure in the direction of the Double K.

Before any more could be said an interruption, in the shape of a fast riding man, stopped the conversation. They all recognized George Lasalle and wondered what brought him into town at such a speed.

''Captain Fog!'' Lasalle gasped, even before his horse slid to a halt. ''Miss Keller came to visit us this morning. Her father thinks he bought all our land. She asked Freda and Morg to go back with her to the Double K house to see and explain things to her father.''

''Dusty's face looked suddenly grim. He turned to the listening men and they saw that he considered the situation to be very grave.

''Mark, Waco!'' he snapped. ''Get your horses. Mallick's headed for the Double K and happen he finds Freda and Morg there all hell's due to pop!''

* Swish: HOMOSEXUAL

CHAPTER FIFTEEN

Mallick's Plan

THE redbone hound raised his head and gave a low growl which caused Morg Summers to drop the hammer, come to his feet and reach for his gun. It made Freda Lasalle lay aside the bowl of peas she had been shelling, while sitting on the front porch, so she could talk with Morg as he repaired a section of the flooring damaged in the fight. Freda threw a look to where her shotgun leaned by the door for she caught the sound of horse's hooves.

"One horse, gal, coming easy," Morg said, but did not relax. He raised his voice: "Boss! We got callers!"

This brought Lasalle to the door of the barn. He stepped from the door and crossed the open to the house, a hand resting on the butt of the Colt in his waistband. On the porch he looked at the other two, then at the dog which, having done his duty in giving a warning, now lay on the porch with an eye on the open house door in case a sudden departure to the safety of his mistresses's bedroom be called for.

"A gal," said Morg, as the approaching rider came into view on the river bank, then turned her horse and rode to where the bank sloped down towards the ford, her eyes on the house.

"And a pretty one," Freda answered.

"Sure. Rides good too," said Morg, his hand going out to gently squeeze her arm. "I bet she can't cook as well as you do. And I never saw a riding outfit like that afore."

Woman-like, Freda's first look had been at the newcomer's clothes. Even at that distance she could tell the clothes were good quality and well-tailored. She had never seen a woman wearing a top hat or an outfit like that worn by the newcomer but grudgingly admitted the clothes looked good and the girl had a figure to show them off.

Sitting her horse with easy grace, Norma Keller rode along the river bank, studying the small house and the three people before it. She reached the top of the slope and rode down towards the water. Then she remembered something the army captain who commanded their escort from Dodge City told her one night. Halting the horse at the edge of the water she raised a hand in greeting.

"May I ride across?" she called.

"Come ahead," Freda answered, watching Norma and seeing the easy way the other girl rode through the water and towards the house.

"Good morning," Norma greeted, halting the horse. "I appear to have lost my way. I saw smoke from your chimney and rode this way. It puzzled me somewhat. Mr. Mallick did not mention that there were any tenants farming on our property."

"Tenants—farming!" snorted Freda, more annoyed because the other girl drew praise from Morg than for any other reason.

"I'm afraid this isn't your land, Miss Keller," Lasalle put in, guessing who the girl must be for he had heard upper-class British accents before.

A slight frown came on Norma's face. "That's strange. I pride myself on being a good judge of distance and I thought I had at least another two miles before I came to the end of our property."

Lasalle saw the light immediately. He also had to admit the girl was a good judge of distance for there would be another two miles or so more—if the Lindon Land Grant covered the area shown on the map he fixed together for Dusty Fog and which still lay in the side-piece drawer.

"I think there's something you should know, ma'am," he said, stepping forward. "Would you come inside please."

"Thank you," replied Norma. "I would like directions to the house though."

"You must have a cup of coffee first," Freda put in, her hospitable nature coming to the fore. "We haven't had a chance to meet you so far."

"Thank you again," smiled Norma. "I think I will stay. I

haven't met any of the neighbors yet. Papa managed to crock his ankle up and we haven't managed to get around much as yet."

She slid down from her saddle without needing any help and, a point in her favor, attended to the horse before she came on to the porch. She looked down at Bugle for a moment and he beat his tail on the porch floor.

"I say," she said. "He's a redbone, isn't he?"

"Sure is, ma'am," agreed Morg. "Real good one, too."

"Papa hopes to bring some foxhound and staghounds from England if the hunting is worthwhile," she replied. "Are there any foxes about?"

"A few," Lasalle replied. "But more chance of cougar, or bear."

"I never thought of hunting such dangerous beasts with hounds," Norma remarked. "It sounds interesting."

The girl's attitude surprised Lasalle and puzzled him. She did not appear to have any idea of the trouble the Double K men caused throughout the Panhandle country. In fact, from the way she acted, she did not appear to know there were other people in the country. Lasalle decided to show the girl the map and tell her how Mallick and his men acted in her father's name. It would be interesting to see her reactions.

With that in mind Lasalle escorted Norma into the dining-room and seated her at the table. Then he crossed to the side-piece and took out a map and a deed box. Norma glanced at the kitchen where Freda had gone to make the coffee and slam things about. A smile crept to Norma's face for she had not failed to notice the other girl's hostile looks and read them for what they were, the jealousy of a young girl very much in love.

"Have you seen anything like this before, ma'am?" Lasalle asked, spreading the map before her on the table.

She looked down at it, then raised her eyes to his face.

"It appears to be a map of our est—ranch," she answered. "But what is this piece marked off for?"

"I can show you better on this map," Lasalle replied, opening the metal deed box to take out and open another map of the area. "This is the correct shape of the Lindon Land Grant. This part down here is not a part of the Grant. There are, or were, four small ranches on here."

Norma frowned. "I'm afraid I don't understand," she said.

"The map Papa received from Mr. Mallick showed that we own all the block of land. I forget how many thousand acres it came to. What does this mean?"

"I think I'd better start at the beginning and tell you everything," Lasalle replied, taking a seat and facing the girl.

Starting at the beginning and hiding nothing, neither making things worse nor better, Lasalle told Norma of the happenings since Mallick offered to buy them out. The girl watched him, her face showing horror as he spoke of one family driven from their home and the other three attacked, brow-beaten, having pressure brought to bear on them to sell and clear out.

Looking at the shattered windows, the bullet holes in the walls and sidepiece, Norma's lips drew tight and grim.

"You mean that my father's employees did this?" she asked. "Attacked your home, whipped that poor chap and wrecked his home?"

"They did."

Strangely it never occurred to Norma to doubt Lasalle's word. She thought of the sullen men at the ranch, of little incidents, like that party which returned late one night cursing and making a lot of noise. Norma fancied her judgment of character and liked this family even though they had not introduced themselves nor she to them.

"Papa and I have only been here a few days," she said. "And with Papa having crocked his ankle he hasn't been able to look over his property. He loathes riding in a carriage of any kind. But he must be told. Would you come with me to the ranch and help me explain?"

"We will," agreed Lasalle.

"And of course Papa will discharge all the men and make restitution for the damage caused in his name," said Norma. "I promise you that not one of the men will remain here when they return from their work today."

"What work's that, ma'am?" Morg asked.

"I don't really know. They all rode out early this morning and I haven't seen anything of them."

Three faces looked at each other, Lasalle, Freda and Morg exchanged glances which were pregnant with expression.

"Morg, take Miss Keller and Freda to the Double K. I'll head for town to warn Captain Fog!"

"Be best!" Morg agreed.

All thought that the hired guns might be gathering to make one last final onslaught on the small ranchers. In that case a fighting force such as Dusty gathered would be of vital importance.

Freda dashed into her bedroom to change for the trip while Morg left to catch and saddle two horses. Lasalle and Norma talked on and the more they talked the more sure of Sir James Keller's innocence Lasalle became.

The door to Freda's bedroom opened and Norma looked towards it, a smile came to her lips.

"I say, that is a fetching outfit," she said, studying the shirtwaist, jeans and high heeled cowhand boots Freda now wore. "I must get something like it. I'm afraid these togs are more suited for a Hunt meet in Leicestershire than for out on the range."

In a few seconds Freda had lost her jealous suspicions and was talking clothes with Norma like they had been friends for years. The girls took their horses and with Morg riding on one side, Norma on the other, Freda headed them in the direction of the Double K house.

Talk passed amongst them as they rode across the range. Norma wanted to know so much that the sullen hard-cases who formed the ranch crew could not, or would not explain. She managed to preserve a nice balance of keeping Morg answering her questions without giving Freda anything to complain about. In fact Freda could tell of conditions in this section of the range far better than Morg. Norma told the other two of her adventure with the cougar and Freda recognized the Kid's description.

When the Ysabel Kid did not return from Bent's Ford, Freda had worried but Dusty and Mark told her not to. They stated flatly that Double K didn't hire a man capable of catching up to, or downing, their *amigo*. Sure the Kid hadn't returned, but most likely he had good reason for it. Red Blaze might need help with the herd, some word from Ole Devil Hardin might have been received, or the Kid might be around, staked out on the plains somewhere, watching every move the Double K made. Their very confidence reassured Freda. From what Norma, they knew each other's names by now, said the Kid had been busy on his way north.

They came to the big old Double K house, a fine, stoutly

built, two story wooden structure strong enough to act as a fort in time of trouble. Right now it looked silent and deserted, a few horses in the corral moving about, but not a sign of life. The bunkhouse and cookshack looked empty, devoid of life, the chimney of the latter showing no smoke to give evidence that a cook prepared food for all hands.

"They're not back yet," Freda said and Norma nodded.

Morg loosened his gun in its holster as they rode towards the house. He felt worried about the emptiness, it did not seem right. He wondered if Norma might be leading them into a trap.

The front door of the house opened and a tall, burly man stepped out, leaning on a cane. He wore a round topped hat—known as a fez or smoking cap in more refined circles—a dark green smoking jacket, well pressed trousers. On one foot was a shining black shoe, the other had bandages around it. His face looked tanned, healthy, but not vicious. It looked very much a man's face and one Morg felt could be trusted and who would make a real good boss.

"Papa!" Norma said, dropping from her horse and going to the man. "I'd like you to meet two good friends, and neighbors, Freda, Morg, this is my father."

"Pleased to meet you," Sir James Keller said. "Come in and I'll see if I can scare up a drink. The blasted cook took off this morning with the others. Don't know what they're playing at."

"They're not playing, Papa," Norma replied seriously. "Come inside. Freda's father told me some distressing news."

The inside of the house still looked much the same as when Lindon owned the place for it had been sold furnished. Freda remembered the library into which they were taken, it looked out on the north range. The window was open and the room cool after the ride. Keller proved an excellent host, he produced chairs for his guests and seated them at the desk.

"Like to offer you something," but I'm not much at cooking," he said. "Do you have trouble with your help, Miss Lasalle?"

Freda smiled at Morg. "If I don't watch him. Morg's our only hand. We don't have a large spread like this, and I'm the cook. If you like I'll throw up a meal for you. I'd like to."

"Then Norma can help you," Keller replied with a grin.

"Time she learned how to cook."

"I can cook," smiled Norma. "It's just that I don't like eating what I've cooked." Then her face lost its smile. "You had better hear what I discovered first, Papa."

Keller threw a look at his daughter's face, then took his seat behind the desk. Norma told what she learned at the Lasalle's house. He did not speak until she finished. Then he slapped his hand on the table top, a hand which looked as hard as any working rancher's.

"I see," he said.

"Wish I did, sir," Morg drawled.

"It's easy young feller, very easy. I was thinking of making a change of scenery. Decided to come out here. I'd been out west three years ago, hunting, and liked the look of it. So Norma and I held a conference and decided we'd buy a place out here. Arranged it through the British Embassy, they contacted various chappies and got wind of the Double K. Felt it might be an omen, two K's and all that, so we said we'd take it. Got it at so much an acre, deuced great oblong of land."

"Only it isn't oblong, papa," Norma put in. "Mallick sold us land which was owned by other people."

"And then he tried to drive us out, make us sell for a fraction of the value of our places," Freda put in hotly, seeing the light for the first time. "So that he could show you the full area you have bought."

"By gad!" boomed Keller. "So that's the bounder's game. I left it in his hands to keep things going for me, after I put down the deposit. It appears he ran it all right."

"But why'd he wire off the Old Trail?" asked Morg. "He must have known that'd make trouble when the herds came up."

"I don't know!" snapped Keller. "All I know is I aim to horsewhip the bounder when I lay hands on him."

At that moment the door opened and Keller started to rise, his face showing anger. Freda's nostrils caught a whiff of a sickly sweet scent she seemed to recognize, one she did not attribute to Norma for the English girl had better taste than use such vile stuff. Along with the others Freda started to turn and a gasp of horror came to her lips.

Mallick stood in the doorway, a revolver in his hand, lining on the men. Behind, holding the fancy Remington Double

Derringer, stood Disraeli and looming over them, empty handed but no less deadly, Knuckles.

"I'm here, Keller," Mallick said.

The men moved into the room, Knuckles leaning a shoulder against the door while the other two stepped inside. Morg stood half risen from his seat, his hand clear of his gun. He was no gun-fighter and his reactions did not have the ability to make split-second moves. Under the guns of the two men he could not take a chance at drawing his weapon and fighting back.

"Drop the gunbelt, cowhand," Mallick ordered. "Kick it this way."

Morg did as ordered. He knew he had no chance but to obey. He felt Disraeli watching him all the time. Felt also that the fancy dressed little man had not forgotten what happened in the saloon. Slowly Morg unbuckled the belt and lowered it to the ground, kicking it to one side.

"Stay where you are, Sir James Keller!" hissed Disraeli. "No heroics or we shoot down the two girls then this man. Ah! I thought that would stop you. You English gentlemen, with your high and mighty code of morals. You would attack us and risk being killed if only your life was at stake. But not to endanger the lives of these others."

"It sounds as if you know English gentlemen," Keller replied quietly.

His words brought a snarl of hatred from Disraeli. "I know you. I know you well. So did my brother. So did my brother Emmanuel. You remember him, Sir James Keller?"

"I can't say I've had that pleasure," replied Keller calmly. "Now may I ask what you want here?"

"We want money," replied Mallick. "The money to complete the sale of this ranch."

"With or without the part you don't own?"

Mallick growled out something in his anger. "So, I thought Miss Lasalle was here for something. It makes no difference. We want every cent you have in the house. And all your collection of jewelry."

"Really?" answered Keller, still as calm as ever.

"Don't fool with us, Keller," warned Mallick. "We've too much at stake to play games."

"We could always let Knuckles have fun with the girls," purred Disraeli.

"One thing's for sure," Morg put in. "You wouldn't have any use for fun with a gal."

Smiling, a vicious smile which did not reach his eyes, Jackieboy Disraeli minced across the room. His hand lashed out, the Remington's foresight raking Morg's cheek and rocking his head back. Morg started to rise and with an almost beast-like snarl Knuckles bounded forward. With speed and agility which was surprising in such a man, Disraeli stepped aside. Knuckle's huge hands shot out, closing on Morg's throat and squeezing.

"Stop him!" Mallick barked out the order. "You hear me, Disraeli, stop him."

At the same moment Mallick jumped forward and caught Freda's arm, holding her as she tried to throw herself at Knuckles. Disraeli looked at Mallick, a slobbering sneer on his lips. Then he gave the order and Knuckles opened his fingers, letting Morg flop back into his chair. The young cowhand sucked in breath and looked ready to throw himself into the attack again.

"Tell him to sit still, Miss Lasalle!" Mallick ordered. "I might not be able to stop Knuckles again."

"Morg!" Freda gasped. "Don't move."

"Look here, Mallick!" barked Keller, standing up and ignoring the gun Mallick swung towards him. "Get this lot over and let's have you out of my house so I can start making up for what you've done to people around here."

"It's just like we told you," Mallick replied. "I want the money you've bought along to complete the purchase of this place and any more you have, as well as that collection of jewelry you own."

"And who told you about that?" Keller asked.

"I did!" Disraeli spat out the words. "I did. To avenge my brother, Emmanuel."

"You seem to think I know this brother of yours," Keller replied, speaking to gain time, in the hope that something might happen to get them clear of the danger they found themselves in.

"You knew him. You and your accursed kind knew him.

You ruined him. You brought him to be hanged. Have you forgotten Emmanuel Silverman. My brother!''

"Silverman," said Keller softly. "Silverman is it. I remember him. Money-lender, owner of crooked gambling hells, sweat-shop owner. I remember him and it is true I helped lay the trap which brought proof of his guilt. And he killed two women trying to escape, shot them in blind panic—"

"Stop!" Disraeli screamed.

"Keep Knuckles back!" Mallick snarled the words out. "Do it, Disraeli, or by God I'll kill him. We want something from Keller and he can't give it to us if he'd dead or unconscious."

For a moment Disraeli stood with his mouth hanging open. Then slowly, with an almost visible effort, he got control of himself.

"You helped hang my brother and I swore I would have my revenge," he said. I learned of your plans to come out here, Sir James Keller. I came ahead. I met Mallick and we managed to get ourselves in, he as Land Agent and I in a saloon. Then we offered this Lindon Land Grant for sale and you took it. Mallick thought only of the profit, his percentage of the sale and the extra for the small ranch properties. I thought of revenge. We sold you several thousand acres of land which did not belong to the Lindon Grant, and hoped to drive its owners out, to sell to you at a profit. I thought of stringing the wire across the trail. Soon the trail herds would be coming north. When they saw the wire they would attack the man who ordered it to be there. And they would blame you for that. I would have avenged my brother."

"In a most courageous manner," Keller replied.

"Cut the talk!" Mallick snarled. "How about that money, or do I turn Knuckles loose on your gal?"

"You're welcome to what money I have," Keller replied. "A matter of a thousand dollars."

"Don't fool with me, Keller!" snarled Mallick.

Keller shrugged and sat at his desk. "I've never felt less like fooling. My good chap, do you expect me to carry the amount this place costs in a valise? I intended to pay for my place, when I was satisfied with it, by a certified order on the First Union Bank in Dodge City. I brought a thousand along as running expenses and no more.."

For a long moment Mallick stared at Sir James Keller who met his stare and then looked away. Mallick turned towards Disraeli and snarled:

"He's telling the truth, damn it to hell!"

"And as for my collection of jewelry, as you call it," Keller went on. "I left it in the bank at Dodge City, in my strongbox. So it would appear that you can't have that either."

Disraeli gave a scream of rage and frustration. The hand holding the Remington quivered. For a moment Keller expected a bullet to slam into him for the man stood facing him and lining the gun. Norma, face pale, tensed, her hands opened and curved into talons as she prepared to try and defend her father. Morg watched this, he knew that the girl would jump Disraeli at any moment. He knew the little fat man would shoot her out of hand, then cut down Keller. There was only one way to stop, or delay it.

"Hey, swish!" he said. "You watch yourself, or I'll let Freda hand you alicking and sh—"

With a howl of fury Disraeli swung around. He seemed ready to burst into tears and screamed. "Get him, Knuckles! Gouge his eyes out!"

Gamely Morg flung himself at the huge man, straight into the huge hands which clamped on to his throat. Morg felt himself lifted and shook like a dog in the big man's hands. Desperately he lashed out a kick at Knuckles, felt his boot connect with the man's shin but Knuckles gave not a sign of knowing it landed. Only his grip on Morg's throat tightened.

Shooting out a hand, Mallick grabbed Norma Keller's wrist and dragged her to him, thrusting his revolver barrel into her side. His move ended Sir James' attempt at opening the top desk of the drawer wherein lay a magnificent ivory butted 1860 Army Colt.

"Freeze, Keller!" Mallick snarled.

His warning went unheeded by Freda. With the ferocity of a bobcat defending its young she threw herself straight at Knuckles. She screamed, although it was doubtful that she knew the screams left her lips. Full on the huge man's back she hurled herself, one arm locked around his throat, the other trying to rip hair out and failing changed to scratching at his face.

Letting out a howl like a fattened shoat that had felt the butcher's knife. Disraeli jumped forward. His left hand caught Freda by the neck of her blouse and dragged at it, trying to get Knuckles free. The buttons on the blouse popped but the girl clung on. Then Disraeli raised his other hand to bring the gun down on to Freda's head. He struck hard but the girl's hair prevented the worst of the blow, even so it knocked Freda down.

Snarling like a wild animal Disraeli raised his hand again. Sir James Keller started to open his desk drawer. His daughter's life lay in the hands of Mallick but he could not see either the girl or cowhand killed in cold blood.

Faintly, as from a long way off, Freda heard words, Mallick snarling a warning, Disraeli cursing her in his high-pitched voice. Even more faintly she heard the thunder of approaching hooves. Then everything went black.

CHAPTER SIXTEEN

Waco's Decision

THE Ysabel Kid felt puzzled as he rode by the side of the leading wagon. By now they were so far into the Double K range that he could make out the empty, deserted look of the buildings, and still no sign of the hired guns who had roamed the range on his way north.

He looked up at Weems and the housekeeper as they shared the wagon's box with the taciturn driver.

"That there's the house, Bill," he drawled. "Looks a mite too quiet for me."

"I'm afraid you have the advantage over me there, Kid," Weems answered as he squinted his eyes and tried to make out more than a few tiny buildings.

Since leaving Bent's Ford on the day after the Kid's rather hectic arrival Weems had changed. With the Kid he acted in a friendly manner and even thawed out to some small extent with the menials, the two grooms, as he called them, who drove the wagons and the 'tween-maid who was the lowest of the low amongst female employees. He still made them keep their places, but he relaxed slightly under the Kid's influence.

Much to his surprise, Weems had found the Kid to be anything but an uncouth savage. True he lacked some formal schooling, but he made up for it in matters practical and there was little he did not know about how to live most comfortably while travelling in Texas.

For his part the Kid found Weems to be far from helpless and a man with some knowledge, even if shy on other vital subjects. He enjoyed the trip down from Bent's Ford and would be sorry to part from his new friends at the end of it.

After another mile Weems could study the buildings. He

grunted as he looked the main house over.

"Not exactly like our country house in Yorkshire," he said. "A sturdy enough structure though."

"Reckon," replied the Kid.

His eyes took in the general deserted aspect of the ranch buildings and he did not like what he saw. Three saddled horses before the front of the main house, a two-horse riding wagon behind the big barn, like somebody didn't want it seen. To the Kid it spelled out but one thing, trouble.

The wagons rolled nearer, coming down from the north towards the buildings. His right hand near the butt of the old Dragoon Colt, the Kid sat relaxed but watchful and alert for trouble.

A scream shattered the air, coming from the big house, followed by more.

"What's that?" Weems gasped.

He spoke to the Kid's back for on the first scream a touch of the spurs sent Blackie racing for the house. As well as he could tell the screams came from the room towards which he now made.

Through the window he saw Knuckles choking Morg. Mallick holding a gun on Norma while Sir James stood at his desk, hand still on the drawer of the desk. He also saw Disraeli drag Freda from the huge man and raise the Remington Double Derringer to strike down at her. Of all the people in the room, the Kid knew only Freda. How she came to be at the Double K he could not guess, who the rest might be he also did not know. He could tell who sided with Freda from how they behaved.

The big white stallion raced towards the house but at the last moment, when it seemed certain to collide with the wall, Blackie turned. The Kid, ready for the turn, left his saddle. He held his Dragoon Colt in his right hand as he flung himself through the air. Hands covering his head, the Kid went through the window carrying its glass and framework in a shattered wreck before him.

He lit down on the floor, rolling like he'd come off a bad one. Disraeli released Freda and allowed her to slump to the ground. Flame spurted from the small Double Derringer and splinters kicked to one side of the Kid's rolling body. He lined the Dragoon and touched off a shot. The bullet ripped into

Disraeli's chest and tossed him backwards across the room. At the same moment violent action broke out amongst the others.

Snarling like an animal Knuckles hurled Morg to one corner and turned to face the Kid who lay on his back, the smoking Dragoon still in his hands. Seeing the huge man bearing down on him the Kid knew his danger. Knuckles might not carry a gun but was no less dangerous for it. His huge hands and great strength along with his beast-like rage, were fully as dangerous as any gun once he got close enough to lay hands on a man.

Only he did not get close enough. The Kid's big old Dragoon boomed out again and Knuckles at last met a force his strength could not withstand. One third of an ounce of soft round lead ball, .44 in calibre, powered by forty grains of prime du Pont powder, drove up, entered his mouth and shattered its way out through the top of his head. the force of the blow knocked Knuckles back so he crashed into the wall and slid down never to rise again.

The Kid's sudden and unexpected arrival took Mallick, Keller and Norma by surprise. Keller thrust back his chair and came to his feet. Mallick turned his gun away from Norma, thinking to line it on the blackdressed shape. Then Norma took a hand, reacting with cool courage even as the Kid's gun cut down Disraeli. She drew back her boot and lashed out a kick, the riding boot catching Mallick on the front of his shin. The man let out a howl of pain, released her arm and staggered back. Norma's face lost all its color as she saw Knuckles take lead. With a gasp she slid to the floor in a faint.

Gun in hand, Mallick still did not make a fight of it. He saw Sir James open the desk drawer and saw the Kid starting to turn. Then he flung himself back through the library door slamming it behind him. He raced along the hall to the main door and spun around to fire a shot. He backed through the main doors, firing again and sprang to the ground outside.

Behind him, from the house, he heard running feet and sent another bullet through the door. From the house sounded a piercing whistle then a voice yelled one word:

"Blackie!"

Hooves thundered behind Mallick. He started to turn and saw a huge white stallion charging at him. Saw its laid back ears, the bared teeth, heard its wild fighting scream. Desperately he tried to turn his gun, he fired one shot which missed.

He never had the chance to fire another. Blackie came at him, rearing high on its hind legs, the fore hooves lashing out. One ripped into the top of Mallick's head, crunching home with wicked force. Mallick screamed once, then he went down under the savage and awful fighting fury of the enraged white stallion.

The Ysabel Kid and Sir James Keller came from the library side by side although as yet neither knew who the other might be. They were not at the front door when they heard the screams.

"God!" gasped Sir James. "What's that?"

"Stay here, friend," replied the Kid who knew all too well what "that" was. "And keep those gals inside."

With that the Kid plunged out to get control of his horse. He hoped that Weems would show enough good sense to either stay well back, or keep the womenfolk to the rear of the building. That bloody wreck on the ground was no sight for female eyes, or male eyes either, happen the man had a weak stomach.

Quickly the Kid quieted his big white stallion, getting the fighting fury out of it. Then he led Blackie around the house and saw the wagons rolling up at a good speed. He went into the saddle in a lithe bound and rode to meet them.

"Take them around back, Bill," he said. "And keep the women out here, don't let them go around front. There's been a mite of trouble."

After entering and seeing the master's library and passing through to the front of the house, Weems decided the Kid had, as he often did, made quite an understatement when he spoke of a "mite of trouble".

Even before the men could do more than take Freda and Norma to another room, they heard hooves. The Kid, gun in hand, went to the front door, followed by Sir James and a shaken, but armed, Morg. They saw three men riding fast towards the ranch house.

"Don't shoot!" Morg croaked, speaking through a throat which seemed to burn red hot. "They're friends."

"I'd never have knowed," drawled the Kid, holstering his Dragoon Colt as he went to meet Dusty Fog and Mark Counter and a tall, blond-haired boy he had never seen before.

In a few moments Morg managed to introduce Dusty and
the others to Sir James Keller and Weems explained the Kid's
presence. Then they went inside to start the work of cleaning
up.

It was two days after the death of Mallick and his partner.
The spacious dining-room at the Double K held a large bunch
of men. Dusty, Mark, and Kid were on hand, Waco, who had
been like a shadow to Dusty for the past two days of wire
removal and starting to clean up after the departed gunmen,
sat to one side of the OD Connected men. Stone Hart and
Clay Allison represented the trail driving interests. Lasalle,
Ralph Gibbs, sitting awkwardly in his chair, and Pop Jones
had been asked to come, along with Matt Roylans and the
Barlock banker. Weems, back to his official capacity, glided
around and served drinks from the stock brought in the
wagons along with much of Sir James' belongings.

"From what Mallick told me," Sir James said. "He
planned to sell me several thousand acres beyond the true
boundary of the Double K and showed on the map I received
from him. I paid by deposit and was to complete the deal when
I'd seen the property. Then he set out to try and buy the small
ranchers out as cheaply as possible or run them out. He did
not expect me for another month, but our ship made better
time than we expected and I brought my daughter ahead with
an escort supplied by an army friend. However I'd managed to
crock my ankle and so could not ride around and that gave
Mallick a chance to force the last three spreads out."

"How about the wire?" Clay Allison asked.

"Bought in my name by Disraeli and put up to try and make
trouble between the trail herds and myself. He hated me for
something that happened in England and helped Mallick
arrange this entire thing. He hoped I would either be ruined or
killed by the enraged trail crews."

"He near on had his way," drawled Stone Hart. "Happen
Dusty hadn't been on hand and seen what was coming off;
well I reckon I might not have stopped to think. You was on to
Mallick from the start, weren't you Dusty?"

"Not right at the start. I guessed most of it when I pieced
together the map I found in Mallick's office, and tied it in with
the hit at the Lasalle house when they tried to dynamite us out.

That meant we'd hit on to something vital and Mallick wanted
us dead before we could use it. Didn't know what part Disraeli
had in it though. We'd sniffed that scent he used in the office
and tied him in with Mallick. So I figured they were trying to
sell land they didn't own."

"Well," said Sir James. "It's over now. Norma and Freda
have both recovered from the shock of what happened in my
study. It was just a bluff on the part of Mallick saying I
intended to take over the bank notes. So he could put pressure
on the small ranchers. Of course I insist on paying for all
damages caused by my men."

"There's no call for that," objected Ralph Gibbs. "They
weren't your—"

"They rode for my brand and ignorance of their actions is
no excuse. I ought to have known what they were doing. By
the by, Ralph, did you and your lady talk over my offer?"

"Yeah. We'll take you up on it. And we both thank you for
making it."

Only Dusty of the others knew of the offer. Full compensa-
tion for his injuries and the damages for his property. Then if
he wished, to sell his land to Keller, and take over as foreman
of the Double K, with a house built on the property. Joyce and
Gibbs discussed the matter at length and decided to give up
trying to run a one-horse spread one step ahead of bankruptcy
and take the security of a good post as foreman of the Double
K.

"The only thanks I'll need, old son," Sir James said with a
grin. "Is that you get this spread working. How about getting
hands?"

Sir James suddenly grinned again and remembered his position as host. He changed the subject and for a few minutes the
men talked over past happenings and future plans. Then the
party broke up for the trail bosses wished to get back to their
herds and the others to their various tasks.

On the porch Sir James Keller shooks hands with Captain
Dusty Fog. Of all the others Dusty had got on best with the
Englishman for they were much alike and, had Dusty been
born in the same circumstances as Sir James he would most
likely have carried the same three letters before his name.

"I owe you a lot, Dusty," Sir James said. "You can rely on

me to keep the Old Trail open. Give me time and I might even make a Texan.''

''Yeah,'' Dusty agreed, shaking hands with the other man while Mark and the Kid waited with the horses ready to ride north once more after the OD Connected herd. ''You might at that. We'll come down this way and see how you're settling in. And don't worry, you'll have hands coming looking for work, maybe even some of the old crew when word gets out. Ralph Gibbs'll pick you good men.''

He turned and went to his horse where Freda Lasalle stood.

''You remember to come in and visit any time you're out this way,'' she said.

''We'll do that, gal,'' Mark promised. ''See you sometime.''

Waco stood by Clay Allison and watched the three men riding away. He felt empty, lost and sick. Some instinct told him that his destiny stood before him. The chance to change from a trigger-fast-and-up-from-Texas kid to a respected man. But he took on with Clay Allison to finish the drive and a *man* did not walk out on his responsibilities just because it suited him to do so. He must finish his drive and hope to meet the man who he now regarded as his idol again.

''Dusty was telling me as how he needed another hand to help him with the OD Connected herd,'' Clay remarked. ''Asked if I could spare one. So I said I'd more hands than I need. Could let one go all right.''

Now it lay before Waco. The chance he wanted. He knew his life would change, his very outlook must change if he rode after Dusty Fog. He knew he would most likely work harder than ever he did with Clay Allison. Against that he knew that he must get clear of Clay Allison, or forever be marked with the CA brand. Sure he might become a tophand, but always folks would say, ''He rode for Clay Allison'' and think twice before hiring him just for cattle work.

For the first time in his life Waco faced up to what he was becoming. Five men died before his guns since he left his adopted home. Five men failed to beat him to the shot in arguments which might have been passed over. Each time the other man asked for death. But there came a time when a man with intelligence asked himself where it all would end.

Waco had the answer. It could end here—or with him riding the same trail as many another fast Texas boy.

He held out his hand to Clay Allison, reading Clay's hope that he would follow Dusty Fog, reading the thought behind it, that Clay did not want Waco to become like him.

"Thanks, Clay," Waco said.

He mounted the big paint stallion and rode after Dusty Fog.